SORCERESS AT WAR

LISA BLACKWOOD

SORCERESS AT WAR

A Gargoyle and Sorceress Tale / Book 4

Lisa Blackwood

Sorceress at War

Gargoyle & Sorceress Book 4

COVER DESIGNED BY: Heather Hamilton-Senter

EDITED BY: Perry Constantine

PROOFREAD BY: Tracy Vandervliet

Special Thanks to Stan H for his eagle eyes.

Print ISBN: 978-1-990608-50-6

EDITION: 10/27/2021

❀ Created with Vellum

BOOKS BY LISA BLACKWOOD

Gargoyle & Sorceress

Dawn of the Sorceress

Sorceress Awakening

Sorceress Rising

Sorceress Hunting

Sorceress at War

Sorceress Enraged

Legacy of the Sorceress

Sorcery & Firedrakes

Scion of the Sorceress

Sorceress Eternal

In Deception's Shadow Series (Epic Fantasy Romance)

Betrayal's Price

Herd Mistress

Maiden's Wolf

Death's Queen

The Prince's Gryphon (forthcoming)

Ishtar's Legacy Series (Epic Fantasy Romance)

Ishtar's Blade

The Blade's Beginning (short story)

Blade's Honor

Blade's Destiny

The Blade's Shadow

First Queen of the Gryphons

The King of the Anunnaki (forthcoming)

The Anunnaki's Blade (forthcoming)

Huntress vs Huntsman (Epic Fantasy Romance)

Master of the Hunt

Night Huntress

Dragon Archer

Soul Mage (forthcoming)

ABOUT THE BOOK

War is coming. The Lady of Battles will have it no other way.

Lillian and Gregory fear the demigoddess is already moving her pawns and dark knights into place, preparing for the first strike. Earth must be ready, but first Lillian needs to ensure that the uneasy alliance between the Fae and the human military does not fail. Every ally is needed if earth is to have any hope of surviving the coming war.

As fate draws friends and enemies closer together, one new player has appeared unexpectedly—Lillian's new doppelganger. She isn't certain if it's pure, old-fashioned jealousy or something more sinister that has her watching the newly cloned Sorceress with distrust, but the fact remains that her doppelganger's allegiance remains mysterious.

For the good of the alliance, Lillian needs to find out if this new Sorceress is on their side, playing for the Battle Goddess, or if she has an agenda of her own—one that no one can predict.

SORCERESS AT WAR

*B*ehind her, the hamadryad's bark creaked softly as it slid back into place, closing the fissure from which she'd just emerged. As she took in her new surroundings, she flexed her toes in the soft grass of the Mortal Realm.

The small glade she found herself in was quiet. The only noise was the soft rustle of her hamadryad's needles as the tree shifted her branches out of the way. Yet, she was far from alone.

Other Fae and mortals looked on, silent and full of tension.

Were they too shocked to speak?

Well, she supposed, it wasn't every day that they witnessed a dryad being born into the world.

She dismissed the other onlookers. Even had they shouted and yelled, or otherwise acted aggressively toward her, she still wouldn't have paid them much mind, considering them relatively harmless in the rich fabric of the universe.

Her attention focused on her gargoyle protector.

He was all that mattered. The one constant in her existence. Presently, he was standing next to her firstborn body, that of a young dryad. Her beloved protector's expression was understandably startled.

She'd surprised him.

A rarity in their long existence together.

Typically, they thought as one mind. He knew what she was thinking long before she acted. But this plan was one she'd only put in to motion a day ago.

Yesterday, when she still thought with the slow, steady determination of a hamadryad tree, it had not occurred to her to give her other half some warning. But then again, perhaps it was for the best. After all, if even the other half of her soul hadn't guessed her plan, then it made it all the more likely that their enemies would not be expecting this either.

As she took her first faltering steps, relearning how to move her new body, memories unfolded in her mind. Oh, yes, she'd had a name. Her beloved gargoyle had called her Daryna in her last life.

She stumbled over a bit of uneven ground and nearly fell. Weakness coursed through her body until she felt as feeble as a newborn foal. That wasn't a surprise. She'd just been born. Unfortunately, there was more to it than that. The dire situation in the Mortal Realm had required her to act, but the only way to do so was to clone her dryad's body to house the soul and power of an Avatar. She'd been forced to grow this body to maturity far too swiftly.

If the inability to manage a graceful walk proved the greatest hardship she had with this body, Daryna would consider herself blessed. Already she knew that her new body wouldn't live more than a handful of seasons. Less if she was required to do too many great workings of magic. Yet it would serve its purpose. After that, her soul and powers as the Mother's Avatar would return to her first-born body and they would become what she'd always been meant to be.

But first, she had much to accomplish.

Clearing a throat that had only known breath for a few heartbeats, she forced her lips and tongue to form words and speak.

"Hello Durnathyne, my hunting shadow."

"My Sorceress," came her beloved's startled reply as he swept down into an elegant bow.

He paused only a moment and then straightened. In three long strides, he was at her side, dipping his muzzle down to her face and curling a wing around her shoulders to act as a ward against the night's chill. Soon his warm, damp tongue slathered across her shoulder, pragmatically cleaning the sticky sap from her body while also showing her a gargoyle's affection.

"I have missed you." He whined so softly that she doubted anyone else heard. Perhaps not even her firstborn body. That young dryad stood unmoving, frozen in shock. When their gargoyle dipped his muzzle down to her neck and lapped gently at her shoulder, Daryna saw a pained expression spike across the other dryad's face.

But her firstborn body recovered sooner than Daryna thought she would. Good. Adaptability was something they would all need if any of them were going to survive the coming war with the Lady of Battles.

"Welcome to the Mortal Realm, Sorceress. I understand it takes some getting used to."

She could hear the raw pain behind those words. It slipped the other's ability to contain and flowed through the soul connection they shared. The young dryad standing across from her thought she'd just been replaced.

Replaced?

What an odd thought.

Daryna shook her head. It was such a strange sensation having two bodies. Three if she counted her hamadryad. At least the hamadryad did not think or sense emotions in the same way the dryad body did. It didn't feel like a separate personality.

However, the other, her firstborn body, already had a well-developed personality. Daryna dug through her memories for the dryad's name. Ah, yes, she was called Lillian. Named after a dead girl by the one she called Gran.

Frowning, Daryna looked to Gregory. He should have been the one to name her. They always honored each other with a new name at the beginning of each life. That they hadn't, bothered her more than she wanted to admit.

At least Lillian had given their beloved a strong name. Gregory of the Livingstone. In her memories there seemed to be something humorous about the name.

That didn't matter at the moment. Now Daryna was more concerned about Lillian's strength of body and mind. She would have many disadvantages to overcome, now that her understanding of the universe was limited without her soul and power of the Mother's Avatar inhabiting her body.

It all seemed truly strange now that Daryna no longer resided inside the hamadryad.

Perhaps Lillian wasn't the only one limited? They would get through this together.

The Sorceress smiled at Lillian in what she hoped was a reassuring way.

She would explain the nature of her task later. There was something else that drew all her attention now.

Allowing her eyes to travel part way down the other dryad's length, she paused at her mid-riff. There was already the slightest swelling of life curving the dryad's belly. A tiny miracle. A child between her firstborn body and that of her beloved gargoyle.

Without a second thought, she called her power to her and examined Lillian to be sure all was well with their little one. At seeing the new life for the first time, her heart beat fast within her chest as excitement rose within Daryna.

So bright. So beautiful was that new soul flickering before her mage-sight that Daryna grinned. A soft laugh escaped her. It was only a hint of the indescribable happiness she felt at knowing she and Durnathyne would finally be able to love and raise a child begotten of their own blood.

While Daryna was momentarily lost in her great delight, Lillian took a couple of steps away. She half turned and then gestured down one of the green, leafy corridors that formed the maze that surrounded the hamadryad tree.

"You must be cold. Come with me. I will show you where you can clean up and find a set of clothing." Another pained expression crossed Lillian's face. "Mine should fit you well enough."

"Yes, I suppose they would." She looked down at her naked body. As Lillian had noted, it was a twin to hers. Once Daryna washed away the sticky coating of a hamadryad's afterbirth and clothed her new body, there would be no physical markers to differentiate them. It was likely adding to Lillian's feelings of disquiet. "I am sorry. I know this must be a shock for you. But once I explain everything, you will understand."

Across from her, Lillian arched an eyebrow in doubt and muttered something under her breath that sounded like 'I doubt that.'

Durnathyne huffed softly, tilting his ears in Lillian's direction. He'd heard the words, too, and held out a beseeching hand. When the dryad didn't come, he tried again. This time he stretched out the wing not sheltering Daryna toward the other dryad.

Lillian didn't accept Gregory's invitation to come closer. Instead, she turned and started away.

"Oh, man," a young human male whispered. "Burn. Gregory, you're totally sleeping on the couch tonight."

Daryna narrowed her eyes and focused on the speaker. After sifting through her new memories, she came to understand this one was Lillian's human brother. He was... unimportant in the grand plan, so she ignored him and focused her attention on the retreating form of her other-self. "Lillian, our beloved Durnathyne still needs you as much as he did before my birth."

Lillian halted and then turned back to them. Her lips parted and she inhaled a deep breath. After several heart-beats, she snapped her teeth back together without saying anything. But Daryna caught the other woman's thoughts.

Ah, while she'd been hurt by their gargoyle's earlier affection toward Daryna, that wasn't why Lillian felt apprehensive. No, the young dryad didn't trust Daryna. That was evident to see in her stiff body language.

In time she would learn that there was nothing to fear.

As her human-raised firstborn body would say, Daryna would move heaven and earth to protect Lillian and Durnathyne.

"His name's Gregory now," Lillian said with an unhappy look.

Ah. Lillian wasn't completely unskilled in magic. She'd managed to pick up on Daryna's thoughts using the soul link they shared.

Daryna raised several layers of shields between them so that once again her mind was hers alone. Lillian and Gregory weren't ready to learn all that Daryna had yet to reveal. In time they would, but not yet.

"You are correct. Our beloved is called Gregory in this life, isn't he? It will take some adjustment, as it always does when we are first reborn, but I will learn and adapt to this life." *And I will always give comfort and guidance to my other half during the coming days which will be both emotionally trying as well as physically dangerous.*

And above all else, I will protect my children. Both that tiny, bright soul nestled in my firstborn body's womb, as well as our full-grown son.

Although, she realized Gryton was likely to be much more temperamental, having been raised by a hate-filled demigoddess.

That was just another one of many injustices Daryna planned to rectify in this life. When she was done, the Battle Goddess would regret ever interfering with the Avatars.

"This way. Before your teeth start chattering," Lillian snapped, drawing Daryna from her thoughts.

When Lillian turned swiftly on her heels and started back down the path, Gregory stiffened. His concern that he had hurt his mate's feelings washed over Daryna a moment later. It was followed by his inability to leave Daryna when she was still so obviously weak.

Ah, yes, if she needed to distract her gargoyle protector from her plans, Lillian would be an excellent distraction.

"It's all right my love," Daryna said. "Go to her. She doesn't understand what's happened. She thinks I'm her replacement."

"But that's ridiculous."

"No. It's not. She's young. And your previous behavior didn't help any either."

"I did not mean..." His ears dropped to half-mast, and his muzzle wrinkled as his eyes narrowed unhappily.

"Yes. I know that, but she doesn't."

"I cannot leave you here in this state." Even his tail

lashed in agitation and indecision. "But I must go to Lillian."

"Well, then carry me. But we should hurry. You're both still wearing those collars. In case you've forgotten."

With a huffing sound that was the equivalent of gargoyle embarrassment, Gregory scooped her up in his arms and broke into long, ground-eating strides. He quickly caught up to his shorter-legged mate. Wrapping her arms around his neck, Daryna rested her cheek on Gregory's shoulder, enjoying the warmth and scent of her other half.

It was nice to hold her beloved close again. She would allow herself to be weak this once. But after tonight she would have to be strong; this life had already proven to be one of her most difficult. Their enemy had already landed too many blows.

Daryna would have to execute her plans as soon as possible to counteract some of what the Battle Goddess had already put into motion.

Gregory might not condone some of her choices, Daryna knew. He might even hate her for a short time.

But once all was said and done with this life, for either good or ill, she could always ask forgiveness when they were reunited again as one being in the Spirit Realm. Until then, she would do what she must to save them all.

If Gregory and Lillian saw her choices as a betrayal? Then so be it.

CHAPTER ONE

*L*illian stomped down the gravel path headed back toward the stone cottage. She wasn't running away. Or leaving in a huff.

'Damn it. Even I don't believe that' Lillian thought to herself.

It didn't matter. She wasn't going back to apologize. There was only so many times she could forgive fate for tossing unimaginable horror into her life. She'd already used her quota of forgiveness. She wasn't going to feel sorry for slighting her replacement. And she'd be damned if she was going to stand there and watch Gregory with his beloved Sorceress for one more minute.

Neither one of them would see her cry. Embracing her anger, she marched back toward the cottage. Somewhere behind, she knew her family and the other Fae followed like some curious parade of bystanders and paparazzi.

At least there were no camera lenses in this crowd.

The only ones were the type found in the scopes sitting atop rifles.

The dark glower of the military was never far. At the moment, she had no desire whatsoever to explain this new...development to the officers or the scientists that had been trailing her earlier in the day.

The present lack of scientists was likely due to her little brother and his pet human. Later she'd thank Shadowlight and Corporal Mackenzie for distracting them. Gran had also been acting as an intermediary, but Anna and the gargoyle child had made the greatest sacrifice as far as Lillian was concerned.

Both had agreed to become the scientists' pincushions, undergoing a myriad of tests. Willingly. Other Fae would always stand guard to ensure that Shadowlight and Anna weren't harmed in the process.

Those stipulations were part of the treaty Gran had managed to hammer out with the military. Personally, Lillian thought it might have had more to do with Gran's persuasive magic than common sense among the humans. Though, no one would tell the military that.

For now, there was an uneasy alliance. Lillian had hoped that hammering out the details of the collaboration would be the greatest stress in the immediate days to come. But no. Fate—that vindictive bitch—had other ideas.

Again, tears threatened to come. Lillian rubbed them savagely away while putting a slightly heavier stomp in each step.

She was nearly back to the stone cottage when Gregory

caught up with her. She side-eyed him. Of course he was carrying his Sorceress in his arms.

Seeing his easy, natural love for her still twisted like a knife in Lillian's heart. Swinging her eyes forward again she locked them on her target. The back-patio door.

"Lillian, please." Gregory's voice reached across the distance, his tones the familiar velvet darkness she'd come to crave. "I am sorry."

Well, I'm damned sorry too. Sorry I wasn't good enough and had to be replaced.

She didn't say it aloud, but by the way his ears wilted back into his mane, she was pretty confident it had shot across their mental link like an arrow from a bow.

Continuing into the stone cottage, she stalked through the kitchen and on into the living room. Behind her, Gregory followed with his Sorceress held in his arms. After that Lillian kept her gaze focused forward as she made her way up the stairs and then down the short hall to her master bedroom.

It was so freaking tempting to simply slam the door in Gregory's face, but she wouldn't be that petty. This entire.... situation...seemed to have come as a surprise to him as well.

Once inside her suite, she went straight to her closet and pulled together a few items for Daryna to wear.

"Take her into the bathroom and show her how to use the shower." Lillian didn't turn from her task. She wasn't ready to see Gregory with her replacement in his arms again. In time she would come to terms with this new nastiness fate had tossed in her path. Lillian drew in a deep breath and silently acknowledged that it would likely take more than a few days. A lot more.

"I do not need help," Daryna said in Lillian's own voice. "I have your memories as well as my own. I know the way of things in this world."

Well, good for you.

Then something else occurred to Lillian. Daryna would have all her memories, not just the small things like how to work a shower or drive a car. Everything.

Daryna would have memories of the few times Lillian and Gregory had been intimate.

She'd be able to experience them like she'd been there.

Lillian glanced at Daryna. If she thought to do more than relive those memories...she'd...she'd...rip the hair from her head and gouge out—

Gregory interrupted Lillian's line of thought. "Daryna, you have much to tell us. You might as well start now while I help you clean up."

"Yes. But it will have to wait. Lillian isn't adjusting well to my sudden appearance in your lives." Pity now marked Daryna's words. "Gregory, she needs you."

Now feeling far too exposed, Lillian steeled her spine and plastered a mask of calm onto her face as she continued to gather a few things for Daryna. "I'm fine. Really. Gregory, of course you need to help Daryna adjust. She can hardly even walk on her own yet. You attend to your Sorceress while I see if I can round up something for her to eat.

Gregory shifted from foot to foot, and his tail flicked with agitation. He was clearly unhappy or profoundly uncomfortable with the situation. It might have been comical if it wasn't happening to her.

"As Daryna pointed out to me earlier, we are still wearing Commander Gryton's tattoo collars. We can't part for long."

Crap, he was right. Damn it.

"No worries. I imagine if I stick my head out the door there'll be a dozen people within shouting distance. I'll get whoever answers to bring us something. I'll be back before the collar has so much as a chance to twitch."

Gregory still seemed reluctant. Maybe she wasn't quite as forgettable or as replaceable as she thought.

Lillian sighed, already tired of the situation. "Go help Daryna."

To end any resistance on his part, she walked out into the hall. It was worse than she'd expected. The hallway was lined with people.

Good God.

She wanted to flee back into her bedroom, but she had a task, so asked for some broth or other light foods. Then she waited with her arms crossed over her chest and locked her gaze on a window at the end of the hall. The window was open, and the night breeze carried the scent of evening blooming flowers.

She fisted her hands and fought against the foolish urge to shift into her gargoyle form and escape out the window. Whatever pain the collars might inflict couldn't be any harsher than seeing Gregory doting over Daryna.

When Gran returned a short time later with a tray of food, Lillian thanked her and then returned to her room.

The lock slid into place with a soft click. She didn't need to turn around. Her ears told her Gregory and Daryna were in the shower. Her eyes slid back to the chair where she had left the change of clothes for the Sorceress. They were still there.

Of course the gargoyle would have forgotten them.

Stomping over to the chair, she scooped them up and then started for the bathroom. The door was ajar, so she took that as permission to enter. Modesty didn't really have a foothold in her mind. The Sorceress wore an exact copy of Lillian's own body. And she'd seen Gregory enough times to be comfortable with him. But once inside the scene still caused a small twist of pain in her heart.

Even though she'd expected it, Gregory stood in the large shower with Daryna supported in his arms. He was helping her scrub the sticky tree sap from her skin. The only reason Lillian didn't turn and flee was because he was all business.

The least she could do was match his brisk, businesslike manner. Continuing into the room, she placed the clothing down on the vanity, and then pulled out a few items that Gregory tended to overlook. Like conditioner. She handed the bottle to Daryna who took it with a slight nod.

Turning away from them both, she left before the shower shut off.

Lillian sat down on the edge of the bed and waited for the other two to finish up. While she waited, she splayed her fingers wide across her stomach. The Sorceress might be able to mimic her to perfection, but there was one thing she couldn't give Gregory.

After what seemed like forever, Gregory exited the bathroom with Daryna. Lillian's clone was now dressed in a pair of her pajamas and had a towel wrapped around her still-wet hair.

Gregory grabbed two chairs and brought them toward the bed. He stood next to the armchair until Daryna settled into it. Once she was comfortable, she began working loose the tangles in her hair. Gregory took the other chair, the one lacking arms, and turned it backward to straddle the seat. Then he looked at Daryna expectantly. "You have much to explain, my Sorceress. Start talking."

Lillian was surprised by his tone. She'd thought he was delirious with happiness to have his Sorceress fully functioning and back at his side. Yet, by his tone, that wasn't the case.

"Indeed, I do have much to tell you and much to accomplish," Daryna said with a slight nod of agreement. "Tomorrow, once I've recovered sufficiently from leaving my hamadryad, I will remove your slave collars. I don't dare wait any longer. If Commander Gryton manages to make it back to the Magic Realm, he will inform the Lady of Battles what has happened. Obviously, we can't allow that."

"Gryton is on the loose again?" Lillian narrowed her eyes. While the battle was a bit of a blur, she remembered one thing in detail. "When you were still in the hamadryad, and I had Gryton under my sword's tip, you saved his miserable life. You said he was needed. Why? What possible reason could you have for wanting him alive? And more importantly—how the hell did he escape you?"

There was a large dose of accusation in Lillian's tone, but given the circumstances, she thought it reasonable. She might not be trained in her magic, but she knew the hamadryad had captured and then transported Gryton somewhere.

"I did save him." Daryna's words were accompanied by a nod, her expression devoid of any guilt. "I am still learning what Gryton is, but already I am confident he is needed, that he has a part to play in the war with the Battle Goddess. The knowledge he has of our enemy and her plans are also something we dearly need."

"But that isn't the full reason." It wasn't. While she could no longer read the Sorceress, Lillian knew it in her gut.

"No. There is also the unfortunate fact that when one of her Commanders is killed, the Battle Goddess senses it immediately. It is better for all if she thinks Gryton still has a chance to capture and return us to her as his slaves. But there is one other reason I did not allow you to end his life."

Daryna paused in her hair brushing and glanced sidelong at Gregory. "Gryton is a fire elemental. He possesses a strength of power that I have never seen. But he is young and lacks full control over that power. If he had died here, there was a chance that he might have burned a huge portion of this world in his death throes."

Lillian's stomach dropped, and her heart did a little skip in her chest. How close had she been to killing everyone in the glade that day?

Gregory jerked to attention with a soft start. "None of

the Battle Goddess's minions are that strong."

"One is now."

Gregory grunted unhappily.

Lillian glanced between them. She did not really know what she could add to the conversation but was suddenly very thankful she hadn't killed Gryton. "But you said earlier that you had to capture Gryton before he escaped to the Magic Realm. What happened?"

"He is a cunning opponent. When I was transferring my soul and power to this new body, he used that distraction to escape. He's since disappeared completely. Perhaps Gregory will be able to track him after I remove the collars."

"Doubtful," Gregory said unhappily. "I've been hunting Gryton since I first learned he had come to this realm, but I have been unable to successfully track him. And I do not believe it was the collars that prevented it. Darkness and Shadowlight also failed to find his trail. Which is unheard of for something to be able to hide its intent from a gargoyle. But this new life seems full of impossibilities."

Lillian watched Daryna and tried to read her, but the earlier connection between them seemed to have faded. Perhaps it was only temporary. Which was regrettable since Lillian would have liked to confirm the truth of Daryna's words.

For now, she would have to take the Sorceress's word in this. Although, that didn't sit well with Lillian since she wasn't at all certain if she could trust Daryna.

That small nagging worry wouldn't leave her.

"What is your purpose?" Lillian asked as she narrowed

her eyes. It was all well and good that the hamadryad thought they needed help, but just what was this clone's plan?

"To borrow one of your phrases, I exist to even the playing field. I'll begin tomorrow by removing your slave collars. After that, we will seek to again hunt down Gryton. And as time allows, I will help Gregory create more weapons with which to fight the Battle Goddess's armies that are sure to arrive far too soon for our liking."

Daryna stood and began braiding her hair. "After that, I will have one other task to perform. Since you are carrying Gregory's child, you will need a hamadryad to gestate our little one. And it is better that the soul and essence of the Sorceress are not residing within the same tree as Gregory's child. Our vows aside, having both Avatars' powers come together in one child would not be beneficial to this world."

Daryna's words might be true, but there was still something...off.

"What else?"

"A selfish want. I have loved Gregory for an eternity, and finally, we have been given a chance to have a child together. I could not pass up the opportunity to help raise our child."

Hold up! The Sorceress wants to raise my baby?

That particular issue hadn't even occurred to Lillian. Well, there was no way in hell. Screaming it at the top of her lungs wouldn't help the situation, so Lillian tried for polite. "You wish to raise my child?"

"Yes. I want to help protect and raise our child for as

long as this body endures." Daryna tilted her head. "I see in your mind that you still view me with distrust. When I created this...clone, I did it to aid you and our beloved. I have no wish to usurp your place."

"I...," Lillian really wished she could read Daryna at this exact moment.

"Lillian, know that I am not your replacement. The way my hamadryad grew this body has severely limited my life-span. A few seasons at most. That's all I have. Less, if I'm required to call on greater works of magic. So, do you see? You have no need to fear me. When this form dies, your soul and powers as the Mother's Avatar will return to you and you shall once again be as you were always intended to be."

Some of the tension eased from Lillian's muscles. This time she detected no hesitation in Daryna's words.

But was it the entire truth?

Maybe. Maybe not.

There was a more important question.

Did she trust the Sorceress with all she held dear?

No.

"In the meantime," Daryna continued as if she was unaware of Lillian's doubts. Although she likely sensed them just the same. "I can help Gregory prepare for battle while you and the Coven act as intermediaries between the military and the rest of the Fae. The humans will have to learn to adapt and work with us, or their entire world will fall with us. There can be no infighting. That is your role. You must make sure there is peace between the humans and the Fae."

"A wise plan," Gregory said, speaking for the first time in several minutes.

Lillian studied him, but he seemed willing to let the two females hash out their differences.

Typical male.

Daryna nodded at Gregory's comment. "We will need all the help we can get. The Battle Goddess has plans upon plans, and her early success in capturing my soul and forcing it to be born in her domain has made her bold. She will act again soon."

While Lillian didn't trust the Sorceress, she was certain she spoke the truth in this. The Lady of Battles was their greatest foe. "I do wonder if the Battle Goddess made a mistake in allowing you to be raised among her minions. You remember what I do not, correct?"

"I do," Daryna said with a chilled smile. "And I intend to make her pay for every little shred of heartache she caused us. The Battle Goddess did not mean for me to ever break free. But I did. Now I plan to use her arrogance and all that I learned while trapped within her domain to crush her."

As much as Lillian did not like it, they clearly needed the aid Daryna was offering. Heavens knew Lillian was mostly useless when it came to magic and spell work.

She simply hoped that Daryna's sudden arrival would be enough to throw the Battle Goddess's plans into complete disarray. Perhaps then the Avatars would defeat their enemy.

That would be the only thing that would make sharing Gregory's affections bearable.

CHAPTER TWO

Gregory was just starting to think that Daryna and Lillian might find a peaceful resolution to this new situation they found themselves in when Daryna yawned and stretched.

"This body is still drained from emerging from the hamadryad," Daryna said. "And I imagine Lillian could use the rest as well. Let us go to bed."

Lillian made a snort that was suspiciously gargoyle-like.

He glanced between the two women, feeling the temperature in the room drop as Lillian and Daryna sized each other up.

The words were badly timed, but in Daryna's defense, not a night had ever gone by that his other half hadn't slept in the protection of his arms if they were together.

Lillian's thoughts came clear to him, and in his mind's eye, he could see her dragging Daryna from their room by her hair.

Oh, for mercy's sake. The Father give him patience.

Gregory stood and held a hand out toward Lillian. "My love, come here."

Lillian glanced away but remained outwardly calm. Only a small flexing of muscle in her jaw and the black nails lengthening the tips of her fingers hinted at the turmoil he felt swirling within her mind and body.

He wouldn't belittle her pain or anger.

In truth, Gregory hadn't expected the hamadryad to act as she had. At first, he was simply so overjoyed to have the other half of his soul housed in flesh and blood once more that he had not thought how his actions would hurt his beloved mate.

But of course, Lillian would not understand and rejoice in a valuable ally gained. He'd been too slow to realize it, and then once he had and tried to reassure her, she'd rejected all his attempts to show her it did not change how he felt about her.

She was his mate. His only mate.

But from the very beginning of their relationship in this life, Lillian had judged herself as flawed because she couldn't remember her past or be who she thought he needed.

That was so far from the truth. Lillian had always been everything he needed. He did not view her as flawed. Her confidence had been building, but apparently not enough to reassure her that Daryna wasn't her replacement.

Gregory could shoulder a lot of the blame for that. He'd handled it poorly.

He snorted a deep huff of challenge. That needed to change now.

One chance. She had one more chance to come to him willingly and then he was going to have to prove to her that she was the center of his being.

"Lillian." He held out a large, clawed hand. Normally she would've come at his gruff call. "Beloved, I'm sorry I hurt you."

"It's fine Gregory. I understand. The hamadryad was trying to help us. And this might be the one thing the Battle Goddess did not foresee."

Gregory's tail flicked lazily as it slowly inched closer to her. She hadn't noticed it yet.

Good.

He would heal all the small hurts he'd caused Lillian if it took the better part of a year. He'd show her that she still meant the world to him. It certainly wouldn't be the first time in this life, or any before it, that he'd made a misstep.

"Strange, I don't remember mentioning the Battle Goddess." Gregory's tail slid across the floor, creeping closer to where Lillian sat staring off toward the hallway.

There would be no more thinking of running away from him after he was done with Lillian. He leaned forward in the chair, his muscles bunching as he prepared to strike.

Lillian must have caught movement out of the corner of her eye because she jerked to attention a moment before his tail struck. But she was too late. His tail wrapped around her lower legs and he launched himself at her.

His tackle was carefully timed to catch her in his arms and roll with her, so she and the delicate life she carried was in no danger of being harmed. His powerful arms wrapped around her and he landed on his back in the middle of the bed.

Lillian's surprised shout was muffled by his wings cocooning them both. A moment later his muzzle was nuzzling the bare skin of her neck and shoulder and then the side of her face. Wherever his muzzle moved, his tongue lapped at her skin, savoring her skin's salty flavor.

When she attempted to kick and punch him, he just continued to cover whatever body part he could reach with sloppy gargoyle kisses. She fought to wiggle free of his affectionate display, but after several minutes she was laughing too hard and gave up the fight.

"I surrender," she said as she draped her arms around his neck and rested her head on his chest.

"Hmmm. Much better," he rumbled happily and wrapped his arms tighter around her. Contentment flowed through his body with each beat of his heart. He smiled into her hair. "Never doubt my love for you."

"I'm sorry for being a needy twit. I think I'm going to blame it on hormones."

Gregory laughed and rested his hand on her belly. His happiness swelled. "Sleep. The morning will be here too soon."

Lillian snuggled closer and soon fell asleep in his arms.

"I'm glad you have found some happiness in this realm."

Gregory glanced over his shoulder to find Daryna

sitting on the edge of the bed. Her hair was now neatly plaited into one long braid. She studied him without a hint of jealousy or judgment.

Muscles in his back that he hadn't even realized had tensed up soon relaxed.

"Is it too much to ask to lie beside you while we sleep? In truth, I do not know if I can sleep without you."

Gregory had been starting to let his guard down, but at her request, he felt the return of his earlier unease. Then a moment later he chastised himself for his foolishness. This was the Sorceress.

"Of course you may rest beside me."

"Thank you, my beloved gargoyle," she said as she climbed into bed beside him.

She snuggled into his back as one arm circled around his waist. Then a brush of warm lips against the sensitive skin between his wings promised trouble for him at a later time.

Some of his earlier contentment dimmed.

CHAPTER THREE

$\mathcal{D}$aryna allowed herself to doze while she waited for Gregory to drift off to sleep. Lillian had already succumbed, but their gargoyle beloved was still trying to be vigilant even though he had to be bone weary. He'd been in an epic fight with Gryton just hours ago, and that offensive collar around his throat had almost destroyed him.

She could still see the delicate tracing of pale lines across his dark skin even after she'd done what she could to heal him while in her hamadryad form.

Sitting up in bed, she stroked a hand along his flank. "Sleep, my gargoyle. I will protect you and Lillian while you both rest and heal."

"I know," he said in a sleepy voice.

Daryna smiled when he relaxed, obeying her gentle command. "That's it. Lillian is safe for now."

Her beloved gargoyle reached back and laid his hand

over hers, stopping its exploring. Daryna lay back down and snuggled into the space between his wings and wrapped an arm around Gregory's waist. She couldn't stay long. There was still too much she had to do before dawn, but she enjoyed the closeness too much to pull away even after he'd fallen asleep.

She gave herself a half hour to listen to his deep, even breathing and then she reached up and placed her fingers against his throat, tracing the tattoo branded there.

While she had been a hamadryad, she'd studied how the tattoos worked. She'd also made changes to them that allowed her to control the hosts. The thought unsettled her, but it would be necessary this night to take control of them while she dealt with another who needed her attention.

It would be only for this one time. After that, she would find other ways to visit Gryton.

"Sleep. And do not wake."

Gregory snorted out a surprised huff, but soon drifted off to sleep again, unable to fight the gentle compulsion.

Next, she reached farther for Lillian's collar. She repeated the same command, and the dryad didn't even stir awake in Gregory's arms.

Once she was certain the command had a firm hold on them both she slipped from the bed.

She needed to have a long conversation with her eldest son.

As she ghosted from the large stone building Lillian and Gregory now called home, Daryna mulled over what she'd learned about her eldest son.

While she and Durnathyne had both been destroyed at the moment of their son's birth and later had their memories wiped upon return to the Spirit Realm, she'd learned Gryton's parentage the moment he'd used her hamadryad to travel to the Mortal Realm.

He'd been unaware what all his unguarded mind had revealed to the hamadryad, thinking her nothing more than a common dryad tree. But as the Sorceress, she'd seen much more than a regular hamadryad.

Now she knew a fair bit about Gryton. Unfortunately, she also knew she couldn't share this knowledge with her gargoyle protector just yet.

While Gregory might not consider the child Lillian carried a blasphemy since she hadn't actually been the Sorceress at the time she'd conceived, it did not mean Gregory would see their eldest child in the same light.

Sacred vows had been shattered to bring Gryton into the universe.

But Gryton was more than broken vows, he was the product of her and her gargoyle's love for each other. It was a forbidden love, but still no less pure for all that.

She refused to believe something born of that pure love could be as evil as they'd always been taught.

When she'd still been a hamadryad, she'd looked into Gryton's mind. On the surface, his thoughts were all cold, hard edges, disdain, and ruthlessness. Under that had been a chaotic mix of desperation, hatred, and despair. Overlapping it all, threads of loneliness and a deep-rooted need to belong had run throughout and interconnected all those other darker emotions.

It was about what she'd have expected of a creature who had been hunted all his life and the only being in the entire universe willing to protect him and teach him had been the Lady of Battles.

But Daryna knew he existed now.

She would protect and guide him while she dug for the good; that potential he'd been born with, that she knew was still buried somewhere deep within. Convincing her other half might take almost as much time and care as teaching Gryton, but Gregory would see the truth in time.

Besides, Gryton was no more flawed than the Twins. And both Lord Death and the Lady of Battles had been created by Divine will and had nearly destroyed the universe in their last fight for dominion.

Gryton's crimes were nothing when compared to the Twins'.

He'd slay a few humans in his quest to fulfill his mission...but their lives were already such swiftly burning embers, what did it matter that a few burned shorter than the rest? Death was just part of existence—had been since the Divine Ones had first commanded their Avatars to birth the Twins into the universe.

What were a few more lives in a world where over a hundred thousand mortals died each day?

If the Divine Ones had cared for all their creations, they shouldn't have sat back and allowed the Twins to wage war against each other. They'd allowed the Lady of Battles to rampage long past when she should have been stopped.

If not for the Divine Ones' misplaced compassion, the Battle Goddess would have been killed long ago so she could rejoin her beloved consort in the Spirit Realm. Perhaps even to one day return to the Magic Realm healed and whole.

But that wasn't Daryna's concern.

As for Lord Death, he'd always been a friend. She would regret having to destroy him as well, but while one twin lived, so too did the other. To kill one, both had to die.

It was part of their birthright, born at the same moment and of the same magic. The duality of the curse that prevented the Lady of Battles from escaping her temple was also powered by the same magic.

But the demigoddess had proven she could manipulate events far outside her own realm, even while still locked within her temple. As a punishment, the duality curse was not enough. She had to be stopped once and for all.

Daryna already knew her other half would not agree, she doubted if Lillian would either. Although, the soul link between them might make Lillian more malleable to Daryna's plans over time. Perhaps.

Caution and secrecy would be best for now. She would study Lillian and Gregory, as well as their new allies to determine if any of them could be trusted with her plans or if she would have to act alone.

If she did have to act out her plan herself, she would still succeed. It would simply take a little longer. In the meantime, if she needed a distraction, she could pit Lillian and Gregory against each other. Though, the idea of setting them at odds sickened her.

They were one being—intended to have one unified

focus, not a fractured relationship that created a divide between them. However, if setting Lillian and their beloved gargoyle against each other was the only way to save all the realms from the Battle Goddess's treachery, Daryna would suffer the pain and do it.

That the Lady of Battles had nearly succeeded in taking command of Lillian using a demon seed only proved how dangerous the demigoddess had become. With or without her allies' help, Daryna would overthrow the Battle Goddess and her twin, Lord Death, replacing them herself if she had to.

As Avatars of the Divine Ones, she and Gregory were certainly capable of filling those roles.

Then she had another thought. Their son might like the chance to usurp the Battle Goddess's throne himself. She could think of none more deserving. If he proved to be what she believed him to be.

CHAPTER FOUR

*O*nce Daryna left the large stone cottage and surrounding gardens behind, she allowed herself to relax and enjoy the walk. She kept the concealment spell wrapped tightly around her body, though. To be discovered now would be...awkward.

She passed all manner of Clan, Coven and military personnel.

Luckily, her spells hid her from view as well as any gargoyle's shadow magic. She continued into the night, following the garden paths to their ends and then farther out into the night-shrouded forest. She still had a couple of hours of darkness left, and Gregory would sleep for at least that long.

Once she deemed herself deep enough into the forest to hide the bright flare of power a transportation spell would release, Daryna called her magic to her. At her summons, a mix of raw spirit magic swirled ten feet in front of her where it combined with the warmer variety born of the Magic Realm.

A shimmering portal formed in the air and she crossed into it and emerged more than three day's walk from where she had started. As soon as she emerged from the portal spell, she could sense Gryton's presence.

Good. He hadn't found a way free yet. That would certainly make it easier to talk to him. Had he somehow managed to escape, at least she'd already drank enough of his blood as a hamadryad to be able to track him anywhere.

But this was better than chasing her son all over the forest simply to have a chat with him.

She started forward again, weaving her way through a pleasantly scented boreal forest until she came to a cliff of rock where the bones of the earth poked up out of the ground. A few thousand years ago, a glacier had slid through the area and then later receded, leaving behind a few hills and valleys and the rocky terrain she now walked toward. She'd stashed Gryton away in one of the natural caverns that dotted the area.

Standing outside the narrow entrance to the cave, Daryna studied the primitive but eye-catching art that some ancient people had once drawn upon the stone walls. But no one had lived here for thousands of years. Well, not unless Gryton counted.

She ventured through the dark, narrow entrance. Squeezing past three separate outcroppings of stone and then picking her way carefully over the loose rubble, she finally emerged into the cavern beyond. The walls continued to widen the further back into the cavern she went.

Overall, one could make a fairly nice home here if one was to put some effort into it. Daryna hoped Gryton would see reason and wouldn't have to stay here too long.

She clambered over a slope where the cavern floor humped up before smoothing into a flat, serviceable area that covered the rest of the cavern. Once she was over the last patch of rough ground, she called to life a glowing ball of light that hovered in her palm for a moment before she sent it floating out ahead of her.

The ball of magic burned like pure fire but needed no fuel beyond her own power. She directed it off to one side of the cavern and then summoned several more of the little balls into being.

The brighter light now revealed her son chained to the bare bedrock by coils of twisting and shifting power. She'd designed the spells to leech energy from him, preventing him from losing control of his magic but also to stop any attempts at escape. Her spells had continued to strip his magic from him until the levels had stabilized.

For now, he was safe, but this intervention wasn't a long-term solution. She'd have to begin teaching her son this night if he had any hope of surviving free of the Battle Goddess's influence, as well as avoiding Gregory's notice.

"I will destroy you. All those you love will know agony. This world will burn with my death!" He struggled, heaving himself a few inches off the ground. The magic tightened, roughly slamming him back down. But it only seemed to fuel his need to escape, and he continued to twist and thrash as he tried to snap the coils holding him.

After a long battle accompanied by snarled curses in a good two dozen languages, Gryton collapsed back to the ground and panted, his fit over for now.

Hmmm. Gryton did not seem like he would be the most willing of students.

Well, she would not be the first mother who had to deal with an unruly child.

She walked around him in a half-circle and then knelt next to him. He uttered something else unpleasant in a guttural tone that was actually rather impossible.

Daryna raised an eyebrow and then chuckled as he continued to spew venomous words at her. "Is that any way to talk to your mother?"

Reaching down, she flipped up his helmet's visor.

Ah. His eyes. Hooded and intense, they were beautiful. Dark, liquid chocolate irises with a ring of flaming amber around the outside glowered back at her. The pupils were vertical, like a cat's. Hmmm. Or a dragon's.

Briefly, she wondered what form her soul had been clothed in when she'd conceived Gryton. Having one's memories wiped was a great annoyance, but one she wouldn't allow to get the better of her. She would recover as much knowledge as she could and put it to good use.

But first, she would just drink in the sight of her and Durnathyne's son.

"You are beautiful," she said and took in the sight of his smooth, pale skin and high cheek bones where they sloped down into perfectly sculpted cheeks and jawline. Presently, his lips were marred by a sneer, which she ignored. From what she could see that wasn't hidden by the rest of his helmet, he possessed a mane, black and thick and sleek, unlike his father's somewhat unruly one.

She fingered a bit that had escaped the edge of his helmet. It was soft. The only softness she could find. His eyes had narrowed dangerously, and his lips pulled back from his fangs. He suddenly drew in a deep breath and a rumble built in his chest.

Daryna placed a single finger across his lips. "Before you try to breathe fire on me, there are a few things I'd like to say, my beautiful one."

Her actions or words seem to surprise him, for he held himself still and watched her with some uncertainty showing in his expression.

"I truly am sorry your father and I could not have been there when you were first born to guide and train you in the use of your powers. The Divine Ones recalled us to the Spirit Realm and wiped our memories within moments of your birth. But I am here now. I will teach you what you need to know to survive and control your power."

To add credence to her words, she waved a hand at the coils of magic holding Gryton down, and they vanished, freeing him. While he was still too shocked by her words and actions to even think to escape, she continued.

"My aid comes freely, and I require nothing of you in return. However, if you come to trust me and are willing to assist me, we can achieve greatness together. If the Lady of Battles is allowed to continue as she has, she will rampage across all three realms until her madness and twisted grief destroys all creation. I do not plan to allow that to happen."

She stood and then held out a hand to him. He stared at her offer of help but did not take it, instead rolling swiftly to his knees and standing without aid.

He towered over her, but she did not feel threatened.

His chest still rose and fell rapidly from his earlier exertions, but he did not attack.

"Why?" The word came out in a growl.

"Why am I willing to help you? Or why am I willing to go after the Battle Goddess?"

Gryton tilted his head and studied her. "Both."

"Because I am your mother. That is reason enough. But if you want more it is also because I think the Divine Ones were wrong in their judgment. My gargoyle protector and I have served the Light since the beginning. We have never served our own desires over the needs of the Light. But in our last life, we chose differently and were punished for our choice. I can see that in your memories."

Gryton took a step back as if that small distance was enough to prevent her from seeing into his mind. It wasn't. "Durnathyne and I chose to create you. I do not know the full reason, but I can guess. Even then we knew where the Battle Goddess's madness would lead."

Her son reached up and slammed his visor back into place and then half turned, like he was planning to leave— or more likely flee.

"You are my son. I fully believe that no child born from the Avatars great love for each other could ever be inherently evil. I offer you my loyalty, love, and knowledge freely.

I will train you. You are not evil, no matter what the Battle Goddess has taught you to believe. You did not choose to be the way you are. You were given no choice. You protected yourself the only way you could, aligning yourself with the only one who would offer you shelter."

He laughed and continued away, heading for the tunnel that would lead to freedom. "I am not some soft innocent in need of your protection."

"No," Daryna agreed. "But you do need training. A great deal more training to reach your full potential and to learn how to hide completely from my other half. Your father is set in his ways. It will take some time before he is ready to meet you."

Gryton halted but kept his back to her. "You would pit yourself against your other half? For me? Why?"

"Because it is a parent's role to raise, guide and train their offspring in order that the young one is skilled enough to survive in the world. But I also believe it is a parent's duty to love their child as well."

"Love?"

His snort of disdain was at odds with the wellspring of need she felt rising from him. Like any child, he'd craved his parents love at one point. He'd since buried that need, but it was still there under layers and layers of disdain.

"However, I do not need to pit myself against my other half in this. He will not need to know this for a while. Only once you are trained, and I have overthrown the Lady of Battles and the Lord of the Underworld, will I introduce Gregory to his son. He will see what I have already seen, that you are not without redemption."

"He's tried his hardest to kill me each time we've met," Gryton pointed out. But Daryna noticed he'd turned and walked back toward her. "Somehow, I don't think the one who sired me will ever greet me with...open arms."

"Not yet, no. But you inherited some of his memories. You know we chose to bring you into being; it wasn't an accident."

"Am I supposed to thank you for starting my miserable existence?" Gryton's tone was incredulous.

"I...do not believe that was our intention." What could she say to that? She had no memories of her own, only those few chaotic ones Gryton had inherited from his father.

"For whatever comfort it gives, I think you meant to leave me a gift of all your memories and knowledge," Gryton said. "You knew you would not be able to train me yourselves once the Divine Ones discovered what you planned. Moments after I awoke and took my first breath, I felt a great spell ripped away from my grasp and shattered across the Magic Realm. Moments after that the first of the gargoyles came to slay me."

Gryton pulled off his helmet and braced one fist against his hip. "I know well what the Divine Ones think of me. And the gargoyle legion. And Lord Death. I don't know why I told you this."

Suspicion entered his gaze.

"I have woven no spell over you. Unless honesty has that same power."

Gryton grunted in a very Gregory-like manner.

But Daryna sensed a softening in his resolution. "One

day, if you're amenable to it, I would like to glean more of our last life from what memories you did absorb before the spell was destroyed. Then, when it is time, I will share them with Gregory."

"Don't you fear what the Divine Ones will do to you? They wiped your memories once."

"Yes. But they did not unmake us. They didn't even demote us, as it were. We are still their Avatars. Perhaps they have allowed us to return this time to do what they themselves could not."

"To kill the Lady of Battles and the Lord of the Underworld? You actually believe that."

"Yes."

"But why should I trust anything you say?"

Daryna stood and raised her arms away from her sides and turned her palms out, showing them empty of any weapon, be it magical or cold steel. "Look within my mind for the truth. I know no other way to reassure you."

She lowered the shields, both physical and mental, that surrounded and protected her.

Gryton's nostrils flared in surprise, but he swiftly stepped up to her and pulled off one gauntlet and then the glove underneath. His strong fingers closed upon her jaw and even as he closed his eyes, his magic reached into her, seeking all that she was.

His soft, quickly drawn breath told her when he found her memories, her present thoughts, and plans. And also, her devotion to him. Family. He was family. The one thing she'd always wanted but could never truly have until him.

After long moments, Gryton released her jaw. His eyes

blinked open, and he just stood, silent and staring for long moments.

"Are you ready to accept my offer of training?"

He sat cross-legged on the floor. Once he was settled comfortably, he looked up at her. "I will allow you to teach me. If you later think to betray me, I will return the favor. What lesson shall we start with?"

"Why, the first one." And so Daryna did, settling to sit cross-legged opposite him.

She had less than three hours to begin his training, but Gryton proved an able student. By the time the sky to the east had taken on a pinkish hue, he'd already learned better ways to harness and control his power without leashing it so tightly that it fought him to be free.

Daryna regretted that her first session with her son was already coming to a close. But there would be other days, although, escaping her gargoyle protector unnoticed might prove difficult. She couldn't risk using the collars a second time. In truth, she couldn't stomach the thought of enslaving Gregory to her will. No. The collars would come off this day.

She would just have to use something else as a distraction. Daryna frowned, not liking where her mind went, but Lillian would be the easiest distraction to use against Gregory if it came to that.

Glancing at Gryton, she said, "If I can't escape tomorrow night to continue your training, take what I've already taught you and reinforce those lessons until they become second nature to you. And think on my plan. I do not require an answer right away."

"I will think upon all you have told me."

She sensed Gryton still didn't entirely trust to the new path fate had set him on, and given his past, Daryna couldn't blame him. Everything that had shaped him reinforced that he could only trust himself. But he was also a creature of logic more than passion, and the intricacies of her plan to slay the Battle Goddess had impressed him.

"Good. Even if Gregory finds your trail and puts a wrench in my plans, I will make certain you don't have to flee back to the Magic Realm empty-handed. But we will talk more on that later. I must go."

"I will be here waiting."

Daryna nodded. He would be. She sensed no deception in his words.

With some regret, she turned from her firstborn son and summoned magic. The portal swirled to life in a vortex of power, and without a backward glance, she stepped through it and appeared in the forest she'd left behind only a few hours before.

She made her way back to the stone cottage and continued inside until she was again looking down at her most beloved other half. She patted him gently and crawled into bed and curled into his warmth.

He slept on, unaware of her treachery.

CHAPTER FIVE

After an awkward breakfast in their room, Lillian again found herself in the company of Daryna and the ever-watchful Gregory as they made their way down to the center of the maze where her hamadryad grew. Daryna had said that she was capable of summoning the magic she would need to remove the collars herself, but that by using the hamadryad to channel the flow of magic from the Spirit Realm, it would be less wear and tear on her new body.

While Daryna had explained the spell work to Lillian, Gregory circled them like an overprotective border collie. Any soldier or scientist who came too close got a warning snarl. Her gargoyle protector had been out of sorts ever since he'd woken up and found he was sandwiched between his mate and his Sorceress.

Lillian might have felt sorry for his apparent confusion if Daryna hadn't been caressing him at the time. Or if it hadn't been equally clear that he'd been enjoying his Sorceress's touch until he saw Lillian's expression. At which point, he'd bolted from the bed like she'd set his tail on fire.

The one saving grace was that Gran was waiting for them just outside the maze's main entrance with a dozen other Fae in tow. The new arrivals gave Lillian someone else to walk and talk with. Thus giving her an excuse to ignore Daryna.

Lillian soon learned that Gran had recruited other Fae in case of trouble with the military or the accompanying science team. In the end, there wasn't any trouble though. Gran's evil eye was more than enough to keep the scientists in check.

If she was given a choice, Lillian preferred the soldiers over the scientists. At least the soldiers only watched them with eagle-eyed distrust. Which was better than being viewed as a specimen for study.

When they reached the center of the glade, they found a good two dozen soldiers stationed inside. Lillian noticed a variety of flags decorating the different uniforms. It looked like half of the world's other militaries had come to join the fun.

"After seeing what one of the Battle Goddess's minions could do all by himself," Gran said as she gestured at the scorch marks that scarred the area, "the joint taskforce has tripled the number of soldiers in the glade in case more enemies than just Gryton came here with him. The military knows the hamadryad is the easiest way to travel between the realms."

"I see the alliance has developed a little more diversity." Lillian nodded to a variety of uniforms.

"It's funny how the threat of a demigoddess from another realm has convinced many of the world's politicians to put aside their petty bickering."

"It's actually reassuring."

"To you maybe," Gran said. "All I see is a big political headache and the likelihood of even more scientists arriving. At this point, even if we devastate the Battle Goddess's armies and win the war, the Clan and the Coven will never be able to disappear into the relative safety of obscurity."

"One problem at a time. At present, I'm more worried about the possibility of more Gryton-type minions arriving than I am of what might happen three months or a year from now." Lillian still remembered all too well the damage Gryton and the collar had inflicted upon Gregory.

Gran sighed. "I'm not even certain who has military command at this point, but I did convince Major Resnick and his superiors to agree to pull some of the soldiers back while Daryna works with the tree to remove the collars." Gran grinned. "Well, convince might be too gentle a word for what I did. There might have been mention of angry demigods should anyone get between them and the hamadryad."

Once they reached the tree, Gran and the other Fae dropped back and stationed themselves around the inside wall of the maze with the military personnel.

Lillian again found herself alone with a stoic sorceress and a watchful gargoyle. While she wasn't happy to be indebted to Daryna, she *was* glad that the collars would be removed soon.

It would also mean that Gregory would be free to call upon his own powers without limit or command. That would be another great weight off her shoulders.

They halted just under the drip line of her hamadryad's canopy. Standing in the shade of her tree's sheltering branches, some of the tension that had lodged between her shoulder blades eased. Her worries were not completely gone, but they lessened as they always did when she was out with her hamadryad.

After a moment, Lillian turned her attention to Daryna, where she'd started to summon magic for a spell.

"When I studied the tattoos while I was still a hamadryad, I learned a great deal about how the spells of enslavement worked. The threads of power linking them to your bodies are easy enough to undo from outside. There were a few other nasty bits of spell work involved, but nothing I can't handle. Although, I will start with Gregory. He'll be able to protect himself better than you would be able to. And while I'm confident, I won't risk our child on an arrogant notion that I know all there is to know about the collars."

Lillian nodded her understanding and agreement. Normally, she would have been quick to volunteer first, but now with the child, she had to be more cautious.

"Gregory, whenever you are ready," Daryna said.

He took a step closer to the Sorceress, and then he knelt on the ground and closed his eyes, tilting his head back almost in supplication. An uneasy feeling rose within

Lillian again. But Daryna merely rested one hand on Gregory's right shoulder while she fingered the tattoo that circled his throat.

She studied it at some length and then Lillian felt a breeze kick up, one that had no natural source. Magic flickered along Daryna's fingers, a barely visible shimmering.

Soon the Sorceress began a chant. It was almost beyond the range of hearing, even for Lillian's gargoyle-enhanced senses. As the chant grew in volume, the breeze the magic had summoned swirled faster. The slight glow around her fingers expanded, throbbing in sync with both the breeze and the chant.

A chilled power Lillian had come to recognize as Spirit Magic caressed her skin, raising gooseflesh in its wake. Soon the chill had spread, filling the glade and dropping the temperature by several degrees.

Frost glinted on Gregory's dark skin, and Lillian winced at how cold he had to be. But then again, he seemed to be enjoying the cold. Gargoyles were odd. Or perhaps it was actually Daryna's touch he took pleasure in.

Lillian frowned, her stomach souring at the thought. But she stomped on that emotion before it could spiral into something darker. She wasn't going to be jealous about her new doppelgänger. It wasn't fair to Gregory to force a divide between them.

Not yet at least. She'd wait until she had something more substantial than just a primal jealousy to go on.

Daryna continued to call power from the Spirit Realm. A vortex of energy now danced around Gregory. It snatched at his hair and clothing. The cross current winds began to moan, high-pitched and eerie. The savage currents picked up bits of grit and gravel from the walkways and tossed them around the glade, pelting anyone in their path.

Protective instincts flared to life within Lillian, stronger this time, and talons erupted from her fingertips. She took a step toward Gregory and the Sorceress just as the chant ended. The sound of the howling wind halted so suddenly Lillian's ears twitched.

"I would never harm Gregory," Daryna said, stepping aside, so Lillian had a clear view of her mate.

Gregory was still kneeling, but he was now touching his own throat. Then as a toothy gargoyle grin spread across his face, he summoned his magic freely, without needing consent or command from her.

He seemed completely unharmed by Daryna's spell work. Grudgingly, Lillian admitted she owed thanks to the other woman for fixing her most grievous error.

"I know you wouldn't harm Gregory intentionally, but I've seen a lot go wrong, too."

The Sorceress nodded. "I understand. Your trust must be earned."

"I'm sorry," Lillian said, "but, yes, it does."

Again, Daryna merely bobbed her head, that annoyingly stoic look back in place.

Gregory stood and whispered quiet thanks to Daryna. Then he gave her a couple of thorough gargoyle kisses before he walked over to Lillian.

She'd never been a fan of the gargoyle way of showing

affection, but now that it was directed at another person, Lillian felt her insides twist with another stab of jealousy.

'*Ugh. Get a hold on that green-eyed monster,*' Lillian muttered deep in her own mind. *'He's just showing affection to the other half of his soul. Deal. With. It.'*

Yah. Right. The pep talk did nothing for her.

Gregory stepped in close to Lillian, blocking her view of her doppelgänger. He nuzzled her hair out of the way and pressed a kiss to her shoulder. His warm breath and scent surrounded her, making it impossible to stay upset at either Gregory or Daryna.

"I will do the spell work to unmake your tattoo," Gregory said as he tapped a finger against her throat. "Daryna will monitor and protect our little one from the power of the spell and any backlash from the collar."

The concept of a child was still so new to Lillian that it hadn't occurred to her that breaking the spell on the collar might be dangerous to the fetus in her womb. The thought of losing that tiny life terrified her. She wanted Gregory's child.

"I would rather allow my own tattoo to remain in place than risk the life of our child."

Gregory rested his hands on Lillian's shoulders and pressed their foreheads together. "As long as I draw breath, I won't allow harm to come to you or our child."

His words reassured her. It was true. He wanted this child. Perhaps even more than she did. He'd certainly been waiting longer.

"I trust you." Lillian glanced at Daryna. "Both of you."

Daryna and Gregory both bowed in the same old-world

style and then began their work. Even before they laid hands on her, Lillian felt their separate powers reach out and wrap around her.

Gregory stood in front. His thumbs pressed gently against her throat, caressing the tattoo with chilling power. Behind her, Daryna knelt and reached around her to curve her fingers along Lillian's abdomen. Warmth seeped into her body, emanating from Daryna's touch. It cocooned Lillian's unborn child in layers of protective magic.

"There," Daryna said. "Our little one is safe."

Gregory huffed an affirmative and unleashed a torrent of energy. Threads of power flowed across her skin; the cold more intense now that she was its focus. The tattoo around her neck flared with a heated warning, dragging a gasp of surprise from Lillian. The spell branded into her skin shifted and heaved like a living thing.

Her fingers flexed and tension raced up her back. Her breathing came in short, choppy pants.

The urge to shift into her gargoyle form clawed at her mind, but she didn't know what that would do to the spell Gregory wove, so she fought the need.

"Shhh," Gregory whispered, bowing his muzzle close to her ear a moment before he began a chant that sounded similar to the one Daryna had used on him.

Then, just like earlier, he ended his chant and a strange wash of power from the Spirit Realm flowed from his hands into her body, taking with it the constraining band of power that had been circling her throat. There was a secondary shift of power and then she felt free, like a weight was lifting from around her neck. Instinctively she reached for her throat and fingered the skin. It felt whole. Clean and unblemished by the tainted collars.

She blinked and stared into Gregory's eyes for a moment. "Thank you."

Then she turned to face the Sorceress who was already stepping away. "And thank you as well. I am in your debt."

Daryna shook her head. "You owe me nothing. Besides, that seems somewhat self-serving."

"Still, thank you for protecting my child while Gregory freed me from the collar."

"I will always protect our child and our mate."

CHAPTER SIX

Gregory hung back and watched Lillian and Daryna. Even though they'd left the maze behind for the gravel paths of the garden, a chill still followed them. Regrettably, this iciness had nothing to do with the magic they'd summoned for the spell work.

The sensation creeping up his spine was caused by another situation entirely, and he even had a word for it —rivalry.

Gregory had the distinct impression he was the bone of contention between these two formidable females. Daryna was all ancient confidence and superiority, which wasn't helping. Lillian, on the other hand, was doing what she could to adapt to the situation without starting a verbal or physical fight. But she was distancing herself from him.

And that was not something Gregory liked. At all.

All three of them needed to work together as one unified being. But Lillian was raised human, Daryna was set in her ways, and he simply wanted fate to find someone else to toy with for a while.

If a compromise was to be found—and one damn well better be found, there was no way he was choosing between his mate and the Sorceress—it was going to be up to him to locate the solution.

"What would you like to see next?" Lillian asked Daryna, her voice colder than magic from the Spirit Realm.

"You as a gargoyle. I must admit, I'm curious. I've seen what you look like in Gregory's memories, but I want to see you with my own eyes. Then I'd like to go hunting with you both before work demands all our attentions elsewhere."

Lillian's hand dropped to her belly. "I've meant to ask, but are we all confident that shape-shifting won't harm the little one?"

Daryna tilted her head and studied Lillian—giving her a look that said she didn't quite believe she'd been asked such a foolish question.

"Not helping," Gregory muttered into Daryna's mind. *"Are you intentionally aggravating Lillian?"*

Daryna arched an eyebrow at him but directed her answer at Lillian. "Have I not said that I would never do anything to harm our child?" Daryna made a vague gesture at the tree line in the distance. "Besides, a hunt will be good exercise. You'll want to stay in peak physical form for the health of the little one."

Lillian's eyes narrowed dangerously at Daryna's tone.

Gregory stepped between them. "We might not get another chance for days. Gran says the military is badgering her. They want us to work with them more closely. I also need to get back to forging more ward-spelled weapons. And we have an army to raise. A hunt sounds good when compared to all that."

"Fine," Lillian growled.

Gregory felt the betraying wilt of his ears as they drooped to half-mast.

Lillian's expression softened slightly, and she rolled her eyes at him. "I could use the exercise of a good hunt. We can walk to the tree line and then I'll shift. No use giving the scientists anymore of an eyeful than they already had." Her expression turned troubled. "It's bad enough that Anna's been forcibly volunteered to be their guinea pig, but I still can't believe everyone is just cool with Shadowlight volunteering for study."

While Lillian's muttered comment inched back over toward more angry and annoyed, Gregory felt a spark of humor at that particular situation. The young gargoyle loved attention, asking questions, and generally getting underfoot.

"The scientists will get more than they bargained for with Shadowlight and Anna. Besides, Whitethorn and Greenborrow are watching over those two cubs."

"Anna will be thrilled you called her a cub. She's older than me by a couple of years."

Gregory huffed again. "You're all cubs in need of training. And I think I need to master the skill of time travel to find enough hours to rub together to complete all my tasks."

Bending down, Gregory nuzzled Lillian's hair when she

continued to look sour. "But those are worries for later. Come, hunt with me."

The hard glint in Lillian's eyes softened further, and she nodded. But a moment later her expression hardened again when she looked from Gregory to Daryna and back again.

"Do you mind if we bring Shadowlight along for the hunt? He's just lost his father, and with River in a coma, he's alone for the first time in his life. He's putting on a brave face, but he's hurting inside. Anyone can see that."

Gregory dropped to all fours and bumped his head under Lillian's hand. Her fingers dutifully rubbed along his muzzle and then up into his mane.

"Of course we'll bring him along," he said between blissful scratches. "He's ours to protect as well."

Daryna nodded. "I agree. Shadowlight is welcome to come, but you forget he is not alone. The cub has his Kyrsu to act as his family now."

Gregory huffed in surprise. He knew Anna and Shadowlight's fates were linked. He could sense that from the moment he'd laid eyes on the human soldier. But a human Kyrsu?

"And what in God's name is a Kyrsu?" Lillian asked with narrowed eyes as she crossed her arms over her chest.

"Kyrsu is the word for 'second' in the gargoyle language. It's also the title of the second in command of the gargoyle legion," Daryna explained.

"That clears everything right up. Thanks." Lillian glowered at Gregory. "When were you going to tell me this bit of news?"

"I've shared very little about my gargoyle brothers, not

because I wish to keep things from you, but because of lack of time," Gregory said, bumping his muzzle under Lillian's hand a second time. When she resumed her scratches, he continued his tale. "You know that unlike me, the other gargoyles were created to serve Lord Death. While I am their leader when we are born into the world as Avatars, the rest of the time the gargoyle legion is led by others."

"They hold the fort for you while you're away."

Gregory nodded. "Yes. They take command from Lord Death directly while we are with the Divine Ones in the Spirit Realm."

"So, there's always someone to keep an eye on the Battle Goddess even if it's not us," Lillian finished for him.

"Exactly so." He nuzzled Lillian gently, pressing his muzzle against her belly, breathing deeply of her scent mixed with that of their child. His heart filled with joy, and he was distracted until Lillian's fingers caressed his horns.

"Anna and Shadowlight.... you were saying." She prodded him back to the tale.

"Hundreds of centuries can go by while we dwell in the Spirit Realm. In our absence, the gargoyles are led by a Rasoren. Its translation means roughly 'prime leader' and Kyrsu is 'second one.' Since I first met Shadowlight, I've speculated that the Battle Goddess was trying to create her own Rasoren and Kyrsu to lead her armies."

"Yes. You mentioned their titles. But we've squashed the Battle Goddess's plan in that regard, surely?"

"Yes. But that doesn't change Shadowlight's future potential. He was bred to be a strong and cunning leader—

one the Battle Goddess intended to use to crush her brother's army. We have diverted the cub's fate. But now he will grow up to lead Death's armies instead. By a strange twist of fate, Shadowlight has already chosen his second in command."

He sensed Lillian piecing together bits of what he'd just revealed.

Lillian laughed. "Anna is 'second one' to Shadowlight's 'prime leader,' isn't she?"

"Mother Bear might be a more apt name," Daryna said dryly.

Gregory nodded agreement. "A standard prime and his second are often father and son, brothers, or sometimes just long-standing friends. But all are formidable warriors. Only the strongest of mind and body are granted the rule of the gargoyles."

Again, Lillian's expression darkened. "At least Shadowlight is safe from what the Battle Goddess would have turned him into."

Daryna shook her head. "You forget. Having rescued Shadowlight doesn't change what he is, what he will grow into. Fate still has plans for those two cubs that even I cannot see. Seeing the future is not a gift the Divine Ones granted their Avatars."

Lillian grunted, apparently not happy about Daryna's words, but not denying them either.

"Even if fate has a dark path for Shadowlight to follow," the Sorceress continued, "Anna, as his second, will be there every step of the way."

Lillian just shook her head. "I don't want to be the poor soul who has to tell Anna her fate is no longer her own."

"I imagine the human already senses that or will discover that fact soon enough." A small mysterious smile graced Daryna's lips for a moment before vanishing.

Gregory wondered at the cause and decided he'd speak more on this topic when he had a chance to get Daryna alone. "The cub's fate will not unfold for years to come. In the meantime, I shall start his training. I'll even start with today's hunt. It will do him good."

For the first time, both Lillian and Daryna agreed on something. Together, hidden by his shadow magic, they sought out the youngest gargoyle.

CHAPTER SEVEN

*M*erciful light. It looked like the seemingly endless, dreary, useless meeting was finally going to be over. Shadowlight's ears perked up. As he listened from his lair under what Gran called a conference table, he heard the humans gathering together their reports and the scraping of chairs as the officers stood.

Earlier he'd squeezed in between Gran and Anna's chairs and crawled under the table for a nap. To keep from getting kicked in the head or some other body part, he'd curled into a ball, practically sitting on Anna and Gran's feet.

It was the sound of chairs sliding back that had woken him. Yawning, he shifted and stretched.

He'd been too wound up from the aftermath of the battle with Commander Gryton to sleep and had settled for following Anna around most of the night. His shadow magic hid him from sight and only Gran, and perhaps Major Resnick knew he was presently under the table.

Resnick was observant for a human and had noted when Anna had shifted her chair enough to allow him under the large table.

"It's settled then, for now," Resnick was saying, "I'll stop by the labs and tell them that they will have a few volunteers coming in shortly."

From Shadowlight's understanding, the scientists had wanted a female and male from each Fae species to study. Gran had—to steal a phrase from Anna—shot that down. Only volunteers would go to the scientists, and even then, there would be other Fae present to make sure no samples ever left the lab.

He supposed it was wise. Blood had power in more than just the Magic Realm. And Gran had muttered something about cloning and immortality.

Shadowlight knew what immortality meant, but he didn't know the word cloning, and none of his father's memories helped either. Hmmm. He'd ask Anna later.

Other conversations drifted around the room, but he focused on Resnick's whispered aside to Gran. "But there will be volunteers?"

He'd made it a question, but Shadowlight sensed it was more of a statement.

"Of course," Gran said with a chuckle. "We can't have your scientists turning poor Anna into a pincushion and draining all her blood, now can we?"

They wished to drain Anna's blood?

Shadowlight growled threateningly as he hauled himself

out from underneath the table.

When he was free, he shoved Anna's chair behind him and stood guard, his muscles bunching in preparation to lunge and his tail flicking with battle readiness.

"Damn it, kid!" Anna hissed under her breath and added a sharp 'Shadowlight behave' for the benefit of the other humans in the room. She grabbed his shoulder, her short talons digging in painfully.

"Has that creature been here the entire time?" Colonel Tremblay asked, his tone hostile.

Resnick cleared his throat. "He came in just behind Corporal Mackenzie and Vivian. Then promptly disappeared into thin air. I assumed everyone saw him pull his vanishing act."

"Your job is not to assume," came the sharp reply.

"Sorry, sir," Resnick said and then added in an afterthought. "I'll see to the young gargoyle's education. He's adopted Corporal Mackenzie as his surrogate parent and looks to her for guidance."

"Good for him. Now get him trained."

"Gentleman," Gran said as she pushed back her chair and picked up her wooden staff. "He's not a dog, and if you try to treat him like one, the demigods will hear about it. I can assure you of that."

Shadowlight knew adopted was something one did to give a person a family after they'd lost their own. The concept worked for Shadowlight. Anna helped fill the void left by the absence of his parents.

Thoughts of his father—a stone statue who might or might not awaken again in some distant time—came to him. And if that wasn't bad enough, his mother was severely hurt. Anna said she was in a deep coma. Focusing on his parents hurt his heart, tightened his throat, and brought the dampness of tears to his eyes.

"It's my fault, Sir." Anna loosened her hold on Shadowlight's shoulder and walked around to stand in front of him. "I didn't think to tell him not to come. I figured it's better than leaving him to his own devices."

More dark looks were cast about the room and aggression scent filled the air, but after another long awkward pause, the one called Colonel Tremblay merely pushed back his chair and stood. "Major, you're responsible for both the Corporal and the gargoyle child."

The comment got a sharp affirmative from Resnick. After that, the meeting room finished emptying until only Gran, Anna, and Resnick remained behind with him.

"Did I do something wrong?" He didn't like the thought of getting his new friends into trouble.

"Nothing you did, kid," Anna said and then ruffled his mane affectionately. "Just human insecurity at its best."

He bumped his muzzle under her hand looking for more scratches.

She obliged as she addressed Major Resnick. "How soon until I report to the lab?"

"You look like shit. Get a couple hours sleep. I'll tell Fleming he can have you after fourteen-thirty. Vivian wants to introduce me to a few of the Clan and Coven council members around thirteen hundred hours and discuss the possibility of training demonstrations. I want you there to help smooth the edges. Gran says the Fae consider you one of theirs now. I'm going to use and abuse that to secure their full cooperation." Resnick sighed, sounding nearly as tired as Shadowlight felt. "The last thing we need is a violent misunderstanding to destroy the fledgling peace treaty while it's barely hours old."

"I'm all for the use and abuse of power in the name of peace," Gran chuckled and patted Resnick's shoulder. "That's why we're going to make a great team. We'll keep all the factions so busy they won't have time to bicker."

Anna snorted and muttered a 'good fucking luck' under her breath that Shadowlight was sure no one was supposed to hear.

He reared up to walk on two legs and followed the others as they left. When he caught up with Anna, he asked, "We make a good team, don't we?"

Anna laughed. "Yeah, kid. We're a good team. Don't worry. I won't allow anyone to separate us."

Warmth suffused him at the fierce undertone of her words. Reaching along the magical tether that had been created when he'd saved her life by sharing his blood, he touched her mind. Her thoughts were full of strength, loyalty and the need to protect him.

Their mental link was growing stronger. So too was Shadowlight's magic. New knowledge awoke daily alongside more of his father's memories. One such piece of information was the awareness he was now strong enough to issue orders to Anna and she would obey.

It was a dark power, one that he didn't intend to use against her, or anyone else for that matter. Yet there was one thing that terrified him almost enough to call on that ability.

A vision of what Gryton had done to his parents flashed through his mind's eye.

He reached out and grasped Anna's shoulder, forcing her to stop and face him.

Before he could stop them, words came pouring out of his mouth. "Promise you won't ever leave me."

Those six words were more than just sounds given meaning. There was a command buried deep within them. One that made Anna stand straighter and the weariness fall away from her features.

"Oh, kid, you have my word." Anna's expression turned fierce. "I'll do my damnedest to protect you and nothing, short of death, will ever keep me away for long."

"I'm glad." Shadowlight felt foolish tears misting his eyes, and he blinked them away.

"That's what big sisters are for, kid."

Shadowlight nodded and broached another topic some-what uncertainly, "Will you come with me to visit my mother?"

Anna's fierce expression turned softer, her dark eyes glittering with some strong emotion.

"Of course I will. We can go now if you like. I can grab a nap later."

Shadowlight nodded, feeling happier. "Thank you."

Anna chuckled and ruffled his mane. "Anytime, kid. Come on." She turned and started away, her long legs carrying her across the distance quickly. Shadowlight dropped to all fours and loped after her.

CHAPTER EIGHT

Anna found herself hesitating at the door outside River's room. Shadowlight's mother was in a hospital bed with various tubes, hoses, monitors, and wires trailing away over the side of the bed. The readings on the monitors meant little to Anna, but she knew this Fae was in a deep coma. What she hadn't the heart to tell Shadowlight was that no one knew how long his mother would remain in one.

It was a miracle she was even still alive.

River had Lillian's magical tree to thank for still drawing breath. But the tree hadn't been able to fix everything that had been broken within Shadowlight's mother.

Her many burns and lacerations had been bandaged until almost no skin showed. What was visible was mottled with bruises. Gran had told Shadowlight that because River had no hamadryad tree in this realm or at least not one old enough to merge with yet, she would have to fight this battle much like a human.

After Gryton's attack, when they'd first treated River, Shadowlight had demanded to stay near his mother while they tended to her injuries, but he hadn't been alone with her like this, with all the monitors and crap. She knew seeing River like this had to be traumatizing to the kid. That's why Anna was hovering nearby. If Shadowlight wanted time alone with his mother, that was all right. If he didn't want to be alone, that was fine too.

"It's okay kid. I'll be right over here if you need me," Anna walked over and dragged a chair from where it was sitting in one corner. She didn't know who had placed it in the temporary hospital room, but it was too small for Shadowlight, so she appropriated it and sat guarding the door to prevent any nosy scientists from harassing the kid.

At least the two sets of Special Forces babysitters that followed Anna and Shadowlight everywhere had stayed outside in the hall.

Shadowlight inched past Anna and closer to the bed.

Outside, Anna heard the soft crackle of a radio and hushed voices, but otherwise, she wouldn't have been aware of the eight guards out in the hall. She and Shadowlight had initially been assigned twice that number of babysitters, but the halls and rooms of the converted community center were too crowded with scientists and equipment as it was.

Besides, as Resnick had pointed out to his superiors, the gargoyles could vanish in a moment's notice if they wanted to. Human soldiers weren't the only ones watching. The Fae council had assigned their own guards as well.

The only difference was that the Fae would back up Anna and Shadowlight if they ran into trouble with the humans.

Anna could almost taste the lack of trust and anti-goodwill flowing through the halls of the building.

Yep. Her new life was going to be so freaking much fun.

While she mulled over her new life, Shadowlight had knelt next to the bed and was stroking his mother's cheek. It was one of the only bits of skin not covered in bandages.

Shadowlight's ears, wings, and tail all drooped in distress.

He whined softly.

"Kid, I didn't know your mother well," Anna began and added a mental, *and I pretty much hated the cast-iron bitch on sight,* "but she is a tough lady. She'll pull through. She's got one magnificent reason to live."

Ears perking slightly, he glanced at her questioningly

"She's got you. You're her reason to recover and she will."

When she looked up into his face, she saw the damp tracks of tears.

"My father had the same reason, but he's not here now. I wasn't reason enough for him."

Dammit. And damn all warmongering Battle Goddesses, too.

"Kid, that wasn't his choice. He would have stayed with you if he could. Don't doubt that for a moment. And Gregory says he may still heal and walk back into your life."

The young gargoyle surprised her by turning and leaping at her.

"What—" He snatched her out of her chair and into the biggest bear hug she'd ever been on the receiving end of, and she'd been on the receiving end of a few. All four of her older brothers were built like linebackers juiced up on steroids, but she'd never felt like a child's toy before.

Shadowlight hoisted her up and proceeded to crush her hard enough that her bones creaked, and all air was squeezed from her lungs. With her feet dangling in the air and her nose getting ground painfully against his sternum, all Anna could do was pat him on the back and pray he'd put her down before he broke her back or smothered her.

"Can't breathe—"

He loosened his hold a fraction, and she turned her head and drew a deep breath and expelled it in a cough. Once she dragged in a few more breaths, she thumped the kid on the back and said, "I know it hurts now, but it's going to be alright, Shadowlight. It's okay to cry."

As if her words were a release for his pent-up emotions, they came flooding out and he did cry; deep shuddering sobs that shook his body. He didn't loosen his hold, and she imagined she might have a few bruises later. But it didn't matter.

She continued to pat him on the back and murmur nonsense. What the hell did parents say to their kids to comfort them? Her mind kept coming up blank. She hadn't even babysat as a teenager.

Finally, she settled for little white lies, telling him everything would be okay over and over.

Eventually, the young gargoyle lowered her back to the ground. He wiped a forearm across his cheeks and muzzle while Anna remembered how to breathe normally.

Feeling like a teddy bear that had been squeezed in a headlock for too long and had her stuffing rearranged, she tried to subtly realign the discs in her spine.

Shadowlight sniffled a couple more times, but the tears had stopped flowing at least. He glanced over his shoulder and then focused back on Anna. "Is it all right if we go somewhere else now?"

"Of course. Are you hungry?" Anna glanced at the clock on the wall. She still had some hours before she needed to meet with her CO again. There'd be lots of time to take a nap after they grabbed a bite to eat. And if she knew gargoyles at all, Shadowlight was probably ready to eat a horse.

Shadowlight's ears perked up. "Do you think Gran has any of her chocolate chip and peanut butter cookies left?"

"What? You mean you didn't eat all of them this morning while you were waiting for breakfast?"

He shook his head.

"Well, by all means, let's see if we can find some."

As it turned out, they never made it to Gran. Anna was leading Shadowlight down the hospital wing when his sister, her doppelgänger, and a sour-looking Gregory all marched down the hall.

Gregory glowered at Anna and Shadowlight's security detail, but his expression softened and brightened when his gaze landed on the young gargoyle.

"We're going hunting before we have to attend to

today's duties. Did you want to come?" He asked as he dropped to all fours.

Shadowlight bounded over to Gregory, and they greeted each other with boisterous gargoyle affection while Lillian looked on with a grin.

As far as demigods went, Anna had decided Lillian and Gregory weren't bad. Lillian ran her fingers through her little brother's mane and her smile stretched wider. However, the clone held herself further back.

Anna wasn't sure what to think about the clone. Actually, that wasn't true. Anna was one hundred percent certain she didn't like her.

The problem was that she didn't know why.

While she'd missed the doppelganger's birth, Anna had been briefed later. Apparently, this Daryna was supposed to contain Lillian's soul and magic; she was in fact just an extension of the other woman. With a mental 'what the hell do I know' and a shake of her head, Anna had shoved the entire strange new development aside for later.

Well, later had just walked up to her.

Shadowlight broke off his play fight with Gregory and turned back toward Anna. "Do you want to come hunting with us?"

She felt a frown trying to crawl across her face. Hmmm, bumping around in the forest on the back of a gargoyle while they looked for deer to hunt in the rain. Not on her life. She still hurt from getting tossed off Shadowlight's back yesterday when he'd jumped a fallen tree on his way to battle Commander Gryton in the glade.

She didn't know the first thing about riding a horse or a gargoyle, and it had been abundantly clear Shadowlight was unfamiliar with carrying a rider.

Apparently, daddy's memories didn't cover all the day-to-day stuff.

She didn't want to hurt Shadowlight's feelings so told a half-truth. "I'm dead tired and need a nap if I'm going to be useful to my CO later. I'll go hunting with you next time." *Once you've gotten some miles on you with a rider that's not me.* "Promise."

Shadowlight looked mildly disappointed until Gregory bumped the young gargoyle in the side. "Come on youngling. I'll teach you the finer points of being a gargoyle mount so that next time when we drag Anna along, you'll have the skills not to kill her." Gregory huffed with laughter. "In the meantime, Daryna will help teach you how to carry a rider."

"Gregory is correct," Daryna said with a grin. "I'm sure Anna will appreciate not being the one to hit the ground every time you take a corner too sharply."

The Sorceress's words were light-hearted, but that annoying worm of doubt burrowed deeper into Anna's thoughts. Perhaps she should go?

Oh, for fuck's sake. He's got demigods looking out for him. He'll be okay.

Anna fought down what was likely just overly protective maternal instincts. Who'd have thought she'd turn out to be the motherly type? With a somewhat fake smile, Anna wished them a good hunt and watched them walk away. When they were out of sight, she headed off to round up some breakfast, clean clothes, and a shower. Anna's personal guards trailed along behind her as that earlier nagging worm of doubt returned and dogged her steps.

CHAPTER NINE

*L*illian returned from the hunt feeling relaxed even though she'd learned Gregory and Daryna would be spending the day together as they worked on strengthening the protections around the hamadryad to prevent other, unexpected Magic Realm visitors from just popping in. While they worked on higher level spells, Lillian would be helping Gran with a different project involving magic. But even knowing that detail, hadn't chased away Lillian's happiness.

Watching Gregory and Daryna teach Shadowlight the finer points of carrying a rider likely had a lot to do with her feelings of good will toward the Sorceress. The exercise had certainly gone a long way to lifting the young gargoyle's confidence and demeanor. Not that Shadowlight lacked confidence, but the hunt helped him feel useful. And that lightened Lillian's own dark thoughts.

Lillian still couldn't bring herself to welcome Daryna

with open arms, but perhaps she wasn't so very terrible either. She'd been kind to the young gargoyle. And she'd even shared stories with Lillian about the Avatars' history while Gregory taught the young gargoyle how to better control and maintain his shadow magic to hide from adversaries more deadly than humans.

Still, some instinct urged her not to trust her doppelganger twin. And there were the times Lillian felt like Daryna was intentionally trying to stir up trouble.

Lillian's conscience whispered that she was just jealous and paranoid, that Daryna hadn't done anything to deserve her distrust.

But now that she had time to dwell upon it, she wondered how much Daryna had been unconsciously shaped by her stay in the Battle Goddess's domain during those first eight years of her life. Eight years was a lot of time to develop a young mind—no demon seed required.

Another dark thought emerged from Lillian's overactive psyche. When all this was over, and they defeated the Battle Goddess, would they just have a new adversary in the form of Daryna?

Lillian wanted to tell herself it was pure paranoia.

For the first time since she'd found out that her hamadryad had taken her soul and her powers of the Mother's Avatar, Lillian wasn't certain she wanted either back. She definitely liked it better when Daryna was a tree.

But could Lillian survive long-term without her soul or her powers as an Avatar?

And what would it do to Gregory?

Lillian didn't know the answer to either question. Even Gregory might not know.

For now, she would do nothing. However, if some evidence came to light, no matter how small, she would act. Lillian also knew she couldn't overpower Daryna in a fair fight. The Sorceress would have knowledge of defensive spells equal to what Gregory possessed.

But Lillian had seen what a few well-aimed grenades had done to Gryton.

If something did come to light, Lillian would share it with Corporal Mackenzie and Major Resnick. Together, they might have the best chance of coming up with a plan to neutralize Daryna, if worst came to worst.

As far as plans went, it was a pitifully weak one. But it gave Lillian some peace knowing that if her suspicions proved correct there would be someone other than Gregory there to make the hard choices.

Lillian set aside her dark thoughts for now. She was supposed to report to Gran and help with brainstorming ways to 'magic-proof' the military's weapons so they wouldn't suffer a magic-induced malfunction during battle.

Given what she'd just been thinking, it might be prudent to have weapons that magic couldn't easily sabotage.

Standing shoulder to shoulder with Gran, Lillian looked down upon a table full of weapons. Greenborrow stood on Gran's other side. Colonel Tremblay, Lieutenant-Colonel

Harmon, Major Resnick, and three other military personnel Lillian had never met before filled in the table's other three sides.

Gran put down a sidearm and hoisted a large rifle instead. Lillian didn't know guns, but she thought it was a sniper rifle. This beast looked badass. Its every line telling anyone who looked upon it that it existed for one reason; to inflict pure carnage upon an enemy.

"It's just as vulnerable to magic as the smaller guns," Gran said with a curl of her lip. "If you'd like me to demonstrate, I'd suggest going somewhere safer. Preferably a place with a nice bulletproof barrier to stop any stray bullets or shrapnel."

Colonel Tremblay seemed equal parts pleased that Gran was willing to demonstrate and disturbed by how quickly magic could render their weapons vulnerable.

"This will be fun." Greenborrow hooted and slapped his good arm against his thigh. "Magic plus propellants always equals a nice boom. However, I must say I'm curious what it could do to C-4 and things with a bigger explosive force."

"Missiles," Gran said nodding sagely. "Those could be defeated if a magic wielder sensed them coming and reacted fast enough to destroy the missile before getting blown to bits."

While Gran and Greenborrow gleefully discussed plans on what they'd enjoy blowing up, Lillian's thoughts turned to the reason for this little session.

While the Battle Goddess and her army had never come up against modern technology before, the Fae and their new human allies couldn't assume the enemy wouldn't figure out that a well-placed energy discharge near live ammo had an explosive effect. If something wasn't done, a simple spell forged by the enemy could ignite ammo cartridges and deliver a devastating blow to whatever earth forces joined the fight.

Gran picked up a grenade next. "I think with a little trial and error, we can find a way to ward-spell them with a type of shielding magic which might 'magic proof' your guns. At least for a short time. Don't expect miracles. Magic and metal never play nice."

"But you think it can be done?" Resnick asked.

Gran nodded. "I certainly hope so, because next time the Lady of Battles sends her goons to this realm, it would be nice to have some effective modern artillery to back us up. A tank or twenty might come in handy."

Major Resnick choked back a laugh. But it was Colonel Tremblay who answered. "Let's start with the guns. If all goes well, we'll see what we can do about larger ordnance."

"Good," Gran said as she picked up a gun and tried to figure out how to release the clip.

Major Resnick did it for her and Lillian noticed the clip was empty.

It wasn't really a surprise. Trust had to be earned. On both sides.

"I assume you have a place for us to work?" Gran asked.

Resnick nodded. "We have a safe room already set up for your use."

Good. Accidentally shooting somebody wouldn't help the newborn alliance.

"Come, Lillian," Gran called over her shoulder as she followed the officers out into the hall. "You too, Greenborrow. And see if you can find Whitethorn. We could use his help with this. Finding a way to anchor a shielding spell to the metal of the gun is going to take a lot of brainpower and a nice big pot of tea."

This was going to take hours. Long hours where Daryna and Gregory would be off working together while she was here. At least they weren't alone. They were working with the banshee, the unicorn, and the pooka.

Sighing, Lillian reminded herself there was lots of work to be done. Now was not the time to be jealous. With new determination, she followed Gran and the others, ready to start working toward a way to inflict harm on the Lady of Battles.

Six hours later, Lillian straightened from where she was leaning over a worktable. Her back protesting, she stretched and stomped feeling back into her feet. Even the aches and pains caused from standing unmoving for so long didn't dull her sense of accomplishment.

Twelve prototype spell-warded rifles now laid spread across the worktable. It had taken some trial and error. And an explosion or two; one she'd triggered herself from behind the safety of a bulletproof barrier. Yet in the end, they now had working prototypes.

As Gran had suggested, finding a way to affix the spell to the rifle had been the most difficult part. The first two dozen tries had all ended with the spell disintegrating where it was attached to the metal. Sometimes the spell would buck and fight before slipping free of the metal and falling away from the gun. Gran had been correct. Magic and metal repelled each other like magnets of opposite polarity.

In the end, it was Greenborrow who said trying to attach the ward-spells to the rifles was too much like trying to saddle and ride a fractious horse. That had given Whitethorn the idea of weaving the ward-spell into a halter or net that could be slipped over the weapons. Once they managed that, a simple trigger spell had been enough to tighten a shielding spell over the rifle like a snug fitting glove.

The resulting product was a rather otherworldly looking firearm. A long green line ran along the top of the gun and down the handle.

Gran said the glow was a result of the ward-spell interacting with the base metals of the weapon. Over time, likely three or four days, the spell would be drained of power. Once that happened, the gun would be rendered vulnerable to magical attacks again. But as long as the spell was active, the rifle and wielder would be protected from magic-induced misfires.

Or at least that was the plan.

"They are not very subtle," Lillian said with an arched brow directed at Gran.

"They're sniper rifles. It's not like they were very subtle to begin with. Besides, the strength of the glow will let the humans know how much longer their weapons will be useful to them." Gran nodded to the ammo cartridges. "Same with those."

"These will take a lot of maintenance." Lillian shuddered at the thought of doing hundreds of these spells each day.

"We can do huge batches and store them away from any metal and then bring them out as needed. Even the weakest of the Fae could trigger the spell once it's placed on the weapon."

Lillian gave the table a skeptical once over. But now that they'd figured out the spell and how to attach it to a weapon, the process was likely to go faster from now on.

Gran left unsaid that this way there would always be a Fae directly involved with the work. And if for some reason these weapons fell into enemy hands or the new alliance went south, these guns would only be viable for a limited time.

The humans were likely to be annoyed by the news, but it was the truth.

"These will still have to be tested in the field," Gran was saying, "but this is a start."

Lillian nodded agreement. "Good. I'm going to see if Gregory and Daryna are finished for the day and then grab some food."

What she didn't say was that it was well past time for her to reclaim her mate's attention.

CHAPTER TEN

As fate would have it, Lillian didn't escape until after Resnick and his henchmen had had all their questions about the new ward-spelled weapons answered to their full satisfaction. Now she waited at the main gate for the soldiers to wave her through so she could go home at last. She refrained from growling at them even though she really wanted to snarl at something.

She was so hungry she could have eaten the pooka.

Finally, the gate slid open and the guards waved her through. While she trudged past them, she cursed herself for walking this morning instead of driving. But in her defense, it wasn't like she could get either Gregory or Daryna into a car to save her life.

Next time she was driving. The Avatars could run along behind.

Now all she wanted was a quiet dinner. With Gregory, if she could separate him from Daryna for a few hours. If her mate wasn't at the house, she'd just park herself in front of the fridge and start eating.

Her stomach rumbled louder at the thought of food. Lillian supposed an increased appetite shouldn't really come as a surprise. Given the opportunity, she knew gargoyles could pack away three times what a human ate in a day. A pregnant female gargoyle might just be able to surpass their male counterparts in that regard.

She crossed the road to walk on the tree-shaded side; the forest's welcoming presence always replenished her reserves. Some of the fatigue was just falling away when movement between the tree trunks drew her eye.

At first, she thought she'd picked up another military babysitter. Then her senses homed in on the other person. Ah. Not military. This person possessed magic.

A moment later the banshee ghosted between the trees, allowing the fading light to catch on the silver comb that held her wealth of hair pinned to the back of her head. She made eye contact with Lillian and then vanished back deeper into the forest. Her soft footfalls continued to rustle the leaf litter. She hadn't gone far, then.

If that was the case, it most likely meant she wanted to be seen by Lillian but didn't want others to know.

Now what?

Then Lillian remembered the banshee had been assigned to work with Gregory and Daryna. With difficulty, Lillian maintained her direction and pace, not wanting to give away the banshee's location in case she was being watched. It was hard, though. Lillian's every instinct was urging her to storm into the woods and find out what concern had convinced the banshee to seek her out in secret.

When the first side road presented itself, Lillian took it. Unhurriedly she walked to the next patch of deepening shadow along the tree line. Once she was in the deepest part, she called her shadow magic and faded from any mortal eyes that might be watching.

She didn't trust her own skills completely, so darted into the forest as quickly as possible. Then she followed where her gargoyle senses led. She found the banshee standing under an oak tree.

After scanning the area to be certain they were alone, Lillian dropped her shadow magic and approached the banshee.

"What has happened? Is Gregory okay?"

"Your avatar mate was well when last I saw him a mere hour ago."

Lillian raised an eyebrow. "Daryna then?"

"She was well," the banshee said, but a thread of fear now entered her voice.

"Go on. We're alone here."

The banshee paced between two trees, too agitated to stay in one place.

That can't be a good sign, Lillian decided.

"Are you aware that a banshee can sense deception?"

Lillian hadn't really thought of it like that, but Gregory had said banshees could sense a truth from a lie. "Yes. Gregory shared that bit of knowledge with me."

"Sometimes our gift is so strong as to be able to read thoughts. Although that is not always the case. Certainly not if the one we are trying to read is a powerful worker of magic. But even so, my kind know when we are being told a lie." The banshee made a frustrated sound. "I wish I had more to tell you, some definitive proof. But I don't. The Sorceress is too strong for me to read her thoughts, but my nature detects something off—a deception when I am near her. It is subtle."

Again, the banshee betrayed her unease by rubbing a hand against her thigh. "Perhaps deception is too strong a word. But there is an avoidance in Daryna. Or there's something she does not want others to know yet. Or...it could simply be her ancient nature. She has lifetimes of knowledge she's been tasked with guarding. Gregory sometimes has that sense about him as well."

"When did you first notice this?"

"From the moment I laid eyes on the Sorceress after she emerged from the hamadryad." The banshee frowned, worry lines marring her smooth, ageless features. "But the feeling was stronger this afternoon when I worked with her and Gregory. What I sense from her is not evil...just a wrongness."

"Thank you for sharing your worries with me." Lillian braced a shoulder against a tree and sighed deeply. It was both a worry and a relief to have another give voice to her fears. She debated what to confide in the other Fae, and then settled on everything. "I suspected my hamadryad of interference even before she cloned me and created this new sorceress."

"What made you suspect?"

"I had Commander Gryton under my sword's point

when my hamadryad spirited him off somewhere before I could end him. When Daryna arrived, I asked her about it, but she said if I'd killed Gryton it might have triggered a fiery apocalypse, but she also said that Gryton was needed, or useful, or some other line of crap I didn't honestly believe. My doubts were further compounded when Daryna said Gryton had escaped."

Lillian glanced down at her fingers. Her gargoyle talons had flexed longer, her body responding to the worry in her mind. She didn't want to say the rest as if uttering the words would make them real, and she very much didn't want it to be true.

"Go on," the banshee urged. "Lies and evasions only weaken our core strength."

"The hamadryad whispered that Gryton was needed, but the more I examine those memories, the greater my unease grows. I don't think the hamadryad was just protecting Commander Gryton. I believe she was protective of him."

The banshee looked about as unhappy as Lillian felt.

"Do you think something of the demon seed survived?" Even as Lillian asked it, she didn't believe it. This — whatever this was — felt different than the demon seed.

The banshee shook her head. "I would have detected evil."

"We need some kind of proof. If I go to Gregory with this now, I'm going to seem like the jealous lover. Not to mention it will tip off Daryna if I say anything to Gregory. We need proof, and then we need a swift plan of action. But even then, we'll need Gregory's cooperation."

Lillian very much wanted her suspicions to be wrong, but the banshee sensed something was off. That made two of them. And she wasn't a believer in coincidence.

But, by the Divine Ones, what could they do against the Mother's Sorceress? Only Gregory was her match. In theory. But would he go against her even if there was proof of her duplicity?

Hell, Earth probably wouldn't survive a war between the Avatars.

"I desperately hope we're both wrong. But we need to watch Daryna while not giving away that we suspect her. If we find something, we'll take it to Gregory. If he can't or won't act, there is one other who might be able to stop Daryna."

The banshee raised a brow in question. "No Fae or mortal has any hope of defeating the Sorceress in a fight."

"No. But a demigod just might. If we find some proof of wrongdoing, I'll find a way to take what I've learned to the Lord of the Underworld."

"You would destroy yourself?" The banshee was surprised.

"No. But I would destroy a flawed copy to protect everything I love in this world." Lillian rested her hand on her belly.

Although without the power of the Mother's Sorceress, Lillian didn't know if it was possible to win a war against the Battle Goddess.

Earth might lose regardless of what path they chose.

Lillian closed her eyes and prayed she was wrong.

CHAPTER ELEVEN

Not long after Lillian and the banshee parted company, Gregory came bounding through the forest and nearly knocked her off her feet with an exuberant greeting. At first, Lillian was afraid Gregory had caught the underlying worry or the direction her recent thoughts had taken, and he'd come to unearth the reason for her distress.

But after his greeting, he showed no signs of suspicion.

"I missed you. When I finished the spell work with Daryna and returned to the house, you weren't back yet." Gregory looked equal parts upset and sheepish. "I should have stayed in contact with you throughout the day."

"It's all right. You've had your plate full these last few days."

"I'm never too busy to spend time with my mate." Gregory nuzzled her and inched closer.

When he reared up and took her in his arms, it wasn't

really a surprise. Lillian's worries fell away for a short time while she returned his embrace.

"What great weaving of magic did you and Daryna create today?" Lillian asked, hoping her question diverted him from picking up her earlier concerns.

"We built two traps. Anyone from the Magic Realm using the hamadryad to travel here will find themselves captured and transported to another holding spell well away from any populated areas. The prison dome now has Fae and military guards watching it."

"Sounds fun."

"And your day?" He asked in a rumbling tone.

"Long," Lillian said with a laugh. "Long and tedious. We've been working on rendering the military's weapons less vulnerable to magical attack. Several of the prototype guns are ready for testing. They'd like to try to shoot us with them tomorrow, I believe."

Gregory laughed. "A new hunting game? And do we get to hunt them in turn?"

Only a gargoyle would think getting shot at was fun. "You'll have to talk to Anna and Major Resnick about that."

Gregory tucked her against his side and curled a wing around her as he called on shadow magic to hide them. Lillian sighed happily. Without Daryna underfoot, it was like old times again. If she wasn't in danger of passing out with hunger, she might have suggested a long walk in the woods.

But...priorities.

"I'm starving. Let's go find something to eat," Lillian said as she urged Gregory in the direction of home.

Gregory wasn't fooled by Lillian's outward calm. He'd felt her soul-deep pain enough in the last twenty-four hours to know of her unhappiness. They were one being, after all. And it didn't matter if she wasn't presently the Sorceress.

She was his mate. They were one in all ways that mattered.

Besides, her scent would have been enough to signal her emotional distress. If he could have changed events and certain outcomes for her, he would have.

What the hamadryad had done by cloning Lillian was beyond his range of experience. And that experience went back to the beginning of time, so surprising him was difficult under normal circumstances.

Humph. Not that much about this life was normal. The most ancient part of his essence and soul whispered that there was a wrongness that needed to be corrected.

Gregory's mind shied away from that disturbing thought as his tail began flicking with newfound unease. He wanted to think he was just feeding upon Lillian's tension but one thing his long existence had taught him was to trust his feelings and investigate the source of unease.

They reached the large stone cottage Lillian called home and entered through the back door, into the kitchen.

Inside they found two bowls of steaming stew with

their names upon them. Literally. There was a folded paper propped against the large bowls that read 'eat these' signed with a J.

Lillian laughed. "Jason made the stew. It's his specialty."

She scooped up utensils, a still warm roll from a covered basket, her bowl of stew, and then started for the table. Gregory stopped her with a tap on the shoulder.

Glancing at him, she arched an eyebrow in question.

"I have spent enough time in the company of others. I would prefer to dine in our room," he said with a sheepish shrug.

It was true. He was also hoping to mend the growing divide between them as well as spend some time getting to know their unborn child. Lillian's scent was already changing to carry the hint of their baby.

It was a marvel he wanted to take time and enjoy. Never had he dreamed this moment would be real.

He dragged in another deep breath and huffed it out a moment later. Something had changed. Lillian's scent no longer was as sweet. There was now an underlying hint of distress.

Small frown lines had appeared between her brows and at the corners of her mouth.

"I would like to dine with you, too," Lillian said and then tried to seem uninterested in the answer to her next question. "Where is Daryna? I haven't seen her yet this evening?"

Ah, so that was what bothered her.

"She said she would meet with Gran and the Fae council. She'll help to round up volunteers to work with the humans," Gregory said as he urged Lillian out of the kitchen and up the stairs before anyone else had a chance to waylay them.

"Shouldn't we help?" Lillian asked, sounding even less enthusiastic than he felt at the prospect of joining in another meeting.

"No."

Once within the sanctuary of their rooms, Gregory stomped over to the closet and pulled out three large blankets. Lillian watched perplexed as he spread two of them in front of the fireplace and set the other aside while he grabbed a few pieces of wood from the rack to build a fire.

In a short amount of time, he had a fire going, the blankets arranged into a comfortable bed, and the food laid out near at hand. With only a slight hesitation, Lillian joined him.

"What is it with you and fire?"

It was still summer, but the night was already promising to be cold and rainy.

"I like its smoky scent and warmth. It reminds me of home. Fire is the one primary element that never fails to comfort me."

Lillian smiled at him. "I like the sound of water, myself."

"I'm fond of water, too. But fire is my favorite element. It might have something to do with that massage you gave last time we reclined by this same fireplace." He grinned, flashing white curving fangs. "I'd be open to a repeat of last time."

Lillian chuckled. "I thought it might be something like that."

He could scent when her earlier reserve melted away to be replaced by a warm, welcoming scent.

When she knelt next to him and ran her hands over his chest, Gregory shuddered and decided dinner could wait until later.

Much later.

CHAPTER TWELVE

D aryna slipped away into the forest a few minutes after the meeting with Gran and the other council members adjourned for the night. They promised to meet the next night again to discuss how the day's events had progressed.

The purpose of the meeting held little interest for her. Although it did present an opportunity she couldn't pass up. She needed some innocuous ways to escape the watchful eye of her gargoyle protector for short times to meet with her son.

Once she was deep enough into the forest, she called her magic and created a portal to carry her to where Gryton waited.

Moments later she emerged onto the stony, needle-covered ground with its pungent evergreen odor. Last year's needles crunched softly under her feet as she made her way over to the cave entrance.

Before she'd made it three steps, Gryton emerged from behind a clump of trees growing to the left of the cave's dark maw. "You were able to escape your other half I see."

"He's distracted for a bit. But I don't dare stay away too long."

Gryton nodded his head and gestured for her to go into the cave.

"Have you been practicing what I taught you?"

"Yes, and I've mulled over more of your plan." He followed close behind as they entered the cavern.

The warm fire-scent she'd smelled earlier was stronger within. She should be focusing on their plans, but her curiosity won out. "I know you're a fire elemental and if I were to guess, I'd say dragon."

Her son laughed. "Besides the Battle Goddess, you're the only one to ever figure that out. There is much talk and many wagers among my soldiers, but I've never taken my true form. I can barely control my power as it is. Shifting to my true form is something I'd only do as a last resort. Both the Magic and Mortal Realm should consider themselves blessed to have never seen that form. Only Lord Death has ever seen it with his own eyes. I was born in dragon form but had to use every scrap of power I possessed to flee from what was hunting me."

"I am sorry."

"Don't be. Had Lord Death not attacked me, I might have retained too much power and lost the war to control it, effectively ending my life before it had begun. So, in a sense, I might have Death to thank for being alive."

"Truly?" Daryna hadn't known that bit. She was still

sorting through and making sense of his memories. But that just reinforced her belief that the Divine Ones had a purpose for Gryton to fulfill.

"Yes, but that's not what you came to talk about this night. And I have a few questions about your plans for Shadowlight."

"Ask them, my son. I will answer them all."

Gregory reclined in front of the fire, staring into the flames with his head propped against his hand. He was now in his human-gargoyle hybrid form. While Lillian was always welcoming of his varying forms, he knew she was partial to his human form mixed with that of his more primal gargoyle nature.

A lazy grin spread across his lips. He was always happy to oblige.

As lovers, they were very new to each other, and he was still learning what pleased her the most. Although, her soft snores that tickled along his shoulder and neck reassured him that he had skills enough to satisfy his mate.

While Lillian slept in his arms, he stayed awake marveling at his blessing. To finally be able to make love to the other half of his soul and not have the act lead to fiery destruction was something that would never get old.

And there was an even greater blessing—a family.

That silly grin was back full force and wouldn't go away. He didn't care.

Oh, there would likely be repercussions in the Spirit

Realm when they shed these mortal forms one day in some vague and future time. But for now, they lived, Lillian was with child, and the Divine Ones hadn't destroyed them.

Nothing should have dampened his joy at this time.

But one thing still did, all the same.

The awkwardness between Lillian and Daryna. He knew once Lillian became the Sorceress, these difficult times would be put behind them, and she would understand it was never a competition between them. He loved them as he always had.

Still, he had to keep them from starting a war between themselves.

Discovering how to go about that was the problem.

But that was an issue for later. He huffed out a deep sigh and then nuzzled Lillian's shoulder. Smiling, he pressed his lips to the soft skin and inhaled their mingled scents. Content, he watched the flickering light of the fire.

Sleep was just creeping up on him when the soft sound of the door opening and closing drifted across his senses. Even before her scent reached him, he knew Daryna had returned.

"How did the meeting go?" He asked without looking away from the fire.

"It unfolded much the way you said it would." The pads of Daryna's fingers trailed over the curve of his arm and succeeded in dragging his attention from the mesmerizing firelight.

Before he knew what she planned, she leaned forward and pressed her lips against his in a kiss that bordered on dominance. Taken completely by surprise, he just lay passive under her. She changed locations, now nibbling along his jawline with softer brushes of her lips and the occasional flick of her tongue against his skin.

Even as his blood surged with heat and another body part awoke eager to serve, a thread of unease was stirring in his mind. He would always love his lady, but this wasn't right.

"So controlled. Hmmm, I used to be able to shatter that iron control. I wonder if I still can?" Her breath caressed his throat a moment before she brought her mouth back to his. Her hands roamed lightly across his chest, making his muscles quiver at the ticklish touch.

Not wanting to hurt Daryna's feelings, he didn't shove her away. Instead, he turned his head and broke the kiss. He wouldn't fool himself, if things had been normal and there wasn't the awkward Lillian-Daryna dynamic, he might have been willing to toe the line and steal a few moments of passion as long as they didn't take it so far as to endanger their sacred vows.

But this lifetime was different.

Lillian was different than any incarnation the Mother's Sorceress had taken in previous lives. He had been seduced by her newness, her uncertainty. As much as he loved his sorceress of old, he loved his new, human-raised sorceress as well.

"We can't do this." He sat up slowly. It wasn't fast enough to disturb Lillian's sleep, but it had the desired effect of displacing Daryna's caressing fingers. He grasped her hands before she could distract him again.

She blinked at him, surprise and confusion in her gaze.

"My beloved gargoyle, I would never do anything to dishonor you or our vows. I was just going to play some of the games like we used to." Daryna fell silent. "I see now that it was not well-planned on my part. Forgive me."

Gregory huffed softly. "It's all right. I, too, have done things that have not been well-planned. We are one. Nothing can change that fact. I would just ask that you have a care about how Lillian will perceive things. She is young, innocent, never having known a mate until me."

"Perhaps you are correct. Already she is confused by her purpose and mine. I will do nothing to bring her or our child further stress." Daryna shrugged. "And however self-serving it might sound, I do have her best interests at heart."

Standing beside him was the Sorceress of old. She did nothing they hadn't done a great many times before. There was nothing nefarious in her actions. It was this world, and all that had happened to him here, that had him out of sorts.

Never had there been secrets between them in their past lives. They were one being in two bodies. Daryna wasn't intentionally trying to unsettle him or upset Lillian. Gregory huffed at his own silliness.

To reassure his other half that all was well between them, he coiled his tail along her legs, the blade-tipped tail tapping playfully against her thigh.

"Forgive me my insecurities, my Sorceress."

"There is nothing to forgive, my gargoyle." Daryna smiled. "However, this body needs rest, and I have never been particular to sleeping on the ground. I'll bid you good night and claim that big bed for myself."

Daryna unwound his tail and gave the end a hard stroke that had his body jerking to attention. "However, should Lillian wake in the middle of the night in the mood for," she paused, the light of challenge in her look as she lazily took in his naked chest and farther down to where the blanket rested low on his hips, "Something only you can give, be assured I will enjoy watching you, my gargoyle."

With that parting verbal gauntlet toss, Daryna turned and made her way over to the bed while Gregory was too surprised to reply.

Her words almost sounded like a challenge. And while Gregory loved a good challenge, this thing between Daryna and Lillian was becoming a distraction none of them could afford.

Inaction on his part wouldn't work if Daryna acted contrary to her word and continued her attempts to enflame him. He hoped it wouldn't come to it, but he would set some ground rules to protect Lillian's feelings and his own honor if he had to.

Gregory settled back and looked up at the ceiling. The position put pressure on his wing joints, but he liked how Lillian snuggled against his side and curved an arm around his waist.

As if his manhood had a mind of its own, it reared to life again. But this time, it felt right. There was no awkwardness or uncertainty. Lillian was his mate. Desiring her was the most natural thing in the world.

Gregory relaxed and shifted closer to her warmth.

While some males might like being pursued by two females, he wasn't one of them. He preferred his life without drama. Sadly, Fate and the Divine Ones delighted in enlivening his existence in such...creative ways.

As sleep drifted closer, Gregory mulled over the worrisome idea that one day he might have to choose between his mate and the other half of his soul. He prayed it would never come to that.

CHAPTER THIRTEEN

The next morning Gregory awoke feeling refreshed and content for the first time in three days. It likely had something to do with waking up with Lillian in his arms and Daryna still close enough to protect. And all the better, neither female viewed him as a prize to be fought over this morning.

He wondered if he'd missed a conversation between the two while he'd slept. That likely should have troubled him, but he couldn't rally the concern at the moment.

Even Resnick's arrival before breakfast hadn't encroached upon Gregory's feelings of goodwill this morning. Resnick had come to ensure that they were going to keep their promises about doing a demonstration.

Gregory was looking forward to this hunt. It didn't matter that it was a game or training session. He was going to hunt down some humans and teach the other younglings the art of stalking prey. All in good fun, of course.

Now, a little over an hour after Resnick had come to collect him. Gregory stood in a clearing surrounded by forest just an hour north of the military camp. They had chosen this place because it was well away from any human civilians.

Lillian stood at his shoulder and watched Shadowlight with a bemused expression. The youngest gargoyle was presently trying to intimidate the other human soldiers gathered around Anna. Resnick and a few other senior officers were likely too close to Shadowlight's 'pet' human for the youngling's peace of mind.

Gregory doubted the gargoyle child even knew he was being too possessive of his new 'toy' and was threatening to test the limits of even Anna's tolerance. Luckily, up until this point, the human had proven very tolerant toward a gargoyle's tendency toward overprotectiveness.

"Should we call off Shadowlight?" Lillian asked with a grin in her tone. "Anna's looking a little frazzled. She's been doing the lion's share of the babysitting."

The original simple plan to field test the new spell-warded weapons had grown into a more complicated affair. Glancing toward Anna, Gregory decided 'frazzled' wasn't the word he would have picked for her darkening expression. Interestingly, it wasn't directed at the gargoyle child. No, Anna's death glare was for three scientists where they were hovering nearby, waiting next to some crates that soldiers were unpacking from the backs of trucks.

One scientist was having an animated conversation with Resnick, while Anna's expression turned even more sour. But the scientists were undaunted by Anna's dark looks and began adhering what he'd learned were some kind of sensors used to record the wearer's life-signs.

While he and Lillian watched the other group, the new, overly optimistic research team leader approached, holding out some of the same patches toward him. By the time the human reached Gregory, he had drudged up the mortal's name. Fleming, or Doctor Fleming as the human insisted on being called.

"If you would be willing to wear these," the male began, "we'd appreciate the chance to collect some data on you to compare to the young one."

Gregory sniffed at the offered bits of metallic patches with their strong adhesive scent and curled his lips back from his sharp fangs. "No."

The scientist paused but held his ground. He turned toward Lillian next, a dogged expression on his face. "Then I'll just…"

Lillian laughed, but there was a sarcastic bark to her tone she'd learned from Anna Mackenzie. "Hell no. I've already had your science team's premium package deal."

With that, she sidestepped the scientist and started toward where the two Fae equines were waiting at the edge of the forest, well away from the humans. Gregory followed, leaving the scientist to mutter under his breath.

They were half way to the unicorn and pooka when Gregory's long strides overtook Lillian's shorter ones. Presently, she was still dryad, although she would need to shapeshift into her gargoyle form for this new game.

Gregory would be lying to himself if he didn't admit he was looking forward to spending time with gargoyle Lillian. Perhaps after this hunt, he and Lillian could split away from the others.

But first things first. Gregory followed Lillian to where the unicorn and pooka waited.

"Are the humans done talking yet?" The pooka's familiar surly tones reached deep into Gregory's mind. *"I'm looking forward to this hunt."*

"This is a wargame, not a hunt. You know that, yes?"

The pooka snorted, lifted his muzzle and curled his lips back to catch some scent. *"If you say so."*

"I do. There will be no hostilities during this hunt. The humans are our friends." Even Gregory could hear the sour note in his voice. The humans might be allies, but it would be a very long time before he called any of them friends. There was too much hate and bigotry. Or simple fear and misunderstanding. They had a long way to achieve enlightenment. Gregory narrowed his eyes, so too did many of the Fae, he supposed.

"I thought the Avatars didn't lie," the pooka continued. *"You like the humans no better than I."*

"I'm willing to like the humans. Well, after they prove themselves trustworthy." Gregory eyed the pooka from the end of his muzzle to the tip of his tail. "You, on the other hand, have a hearty disdain for all other creatures."

"True," the pooka agreed, his yellow eyes glowing with humor.

Lillian reached out and scratched the black pony's neck. Gregory grinned at the equine's sudden goofy look.

Maybe the pooka didn't hate everyone. Perhaps he'd even trust Lillian enough to share his true name with her one day.

As an Avatar, Gregory could use spirit magic and read everything about the pooka, but to do so would be a violation in the eyes of the Divine Ones. Both mortals and immortals were granted free will at their creation. To know an immortal's true name was to hold power over them, power that could be used to curtail their free will. Hence, why Gregory would never force any Fae to share their true names.

Some Fae were so suspicious, like the pooka, that they wouldn't even take a secondary name for fear that the name could be used to bind them.

Gregory wasn't overly worried about the pooka, though. Of all the Fae, he was the most honest about his motives. He loved the hunt. And he would kill an enemy without a twinge of guilt marring his conscience later.

"I know a secluded glade that isn't far from here." The pooka's mental statement was meant for Lillian alone, but Gregory picked up on it. After last night, her mind was open to him again.

Their time of intimacy had strengthened the blood bond between Lillian and himself once more. Her thoughts were ever present in the back of his mind. All he had to do was reach for them. His were the same for her to read if she so chose.

He'd missed their closeness and didn't plan to allow anything to come between them again.

Not even a black, evil tempered little pony.

"Nice try, but my mate isn't going to be stripping down in front of you."

The pooka snorted in surprise. *"Lillian is lovely, but she is not my type."*

Gregory's mind was just starting to speculate on the pooka's type when his yellow eyes locked on Gran as she approached.

Ah. So that was the way of it. Not that it was really a surprise. Even though everyone called Vivian by the nickname Gran, she was still an elegant looking woman in the prime of life.

"I should shift," Lillian said, drawing his attention back to her. "I see Daryna headed this way. I think the impromptu meeting is over."

At her words, the pooka glanced up at the newcomers.

"That's too many humans for me. I'm out. But I will meet you deeper in the forest." The pooka started away then paused and turned his head to glance back at Gregory. *"Beware gargoyle. I think this wargame might be more of a hunt than a game."*

With that ambiguous warning, the yellow-eyed pony turned and trotted off, his tail flagged out behind him.

Unease penetrated Gregory's earlier enthusiasm. Yet he wasn't so naïve as to fully trust the humans. Still, he would heed the pooka's warning.

Daryna joined them, her power as the Mother's Sorceress washing along his senses even before she'd stopped at his side.

"I think the humans are almost ready."

Again there was that mild note of disdain for the

mortals. Gregory couldn't pass judgment, though. In his darker moments, he'd had similar emotions regarding this modern world.

"Well, let's get this show on the road," Lillian said and gestured toward the path the pooka had taken. Gregory dropped to all fours and loped alongside Lillian. Daryna fell in on his other side.

"The pooka knows a small clearing where Lillian can shapeshift away from the scientists," Gregory explained to Daryna.

"Good. Those scientists seem...eager."

Gregory huffed in humor and Lillian echoed his thoughts for him. "You're too polite."

They made the rest of the short journey in silence and soon reached the spot the pooka had scouted out earlier. It was blessedly free of the noise and strange scents of technology. Here the forest creatures still went about their business, undisturbed by the humans he could still hear in the distance.

"This will do," Lillian said as she tugged off her outer clothing. Underneath she was wearing the ward-spelled garments he'd created to shapeshift with her.

She dropped to all fours as magic flickered along her body. The familiar power shimmered brighter, and then wings emerged from her back. Moments after, horns thrust up from her hairline. Then in a blur too fast to follow, his dryad beloved vanished, replaced by gargoyle Lillian.

She gave her wings and tail a shake and then straightened, her muzzle curling back as she caught his scent.

"Hmmm, you still smell far too good," Lillian said with a hiss. "Am I ever going to get used to that?"

Gregory gave her a toothy gargoyle grin. "I hope not."

Bounding across the small distance, he bumped his muzzle under her hand as he dragged in a deeper breath of her scent.

"Our gargoyle form is magnificent," Daryna said as she looked Lillian over. "While I do not enjoy the Battle Goddess's manipulations, I cannot fault her taste in design. You make a beautiful gargoyle."

Lillian studied Daryna silently and then glanced at Gregory. He sensed some unknown emotion flowed between the two women, but they were both now shielding their thoughts. Before he could dig deeper, Anna came tromping up to them. Shadowlight was running circles around her in a playful abandon, and the one-horned fool was bringing up the rear of their little caravan.

"All teams are in place. We are ready to start," Anna announced to the group at large and then she glanced pointedly at Daryna. "Gran and Resnick said you were going to watch from the sidelines, showing them some magic real-time surveillance spell thing."

"I did. And now that I've seen my new gargoyle self with my own eyes, I'll return to Vivian and Resnick," Daryna said with a placid nod of her head. "And if the unicorn would be so gallant as to offer me a ride, it would save some time."

The unicorn danced in place, his body language saying he'd rather take part in the hunt than act the part of faithful mount, but he obeyed Daryna's request and sidled up beside her to offer his back.

With a gracious nod, Daryna grabbed a fistful of the unicorn's mane and leaped up onto his back. Once she was astride, the unicorn arched his neck and neighed a challenge at the other males before he galloped away.

Gregory glowered at the flashing hooves as they retreated down the game trail.

"What was that all about?" Lillian asked with an arched brow.

"Male posturing," Gregory answered honestly.

Anna cleared her throat. "Unicorn posturing? Alrighty. On that note...let's get to work."

Gregory nodded sharply, and Anna's expression turned serious.

"The name of the game is to run through a simulated warzone and reach the extraction point fifty kilometers due north of here. All without getting detected."

"Fifty kilometers? Are we running an Ironman?" Lillian asked.

"Not even close," Anna laughed. "Think of this as a BFT."

Lillian's ears pinned to her mane and Gregory bumped her flank. A moment later, they relaxed, and she snorted with humor. "Let me guess. A BFT isn't a sandwich. I'd be all kinds of down with a sandwich..."

"Gargoyles." Anna rolled her eyes. "BFT...battle fitness test. Major Resnick wants to know exactly what you're capable of."

Shadowlight shoved his nose against Anna's rucksack. "She does have food in here. I can smell it."

"Rations are for later." The human shooed the young gargoyle away. "If you care to know, you have Gran and Greenborrow's input to thank for the length of the run. They said anything less would be an insult to a gargoyle's speed and stamina. For the record, I'm totally going to have to ride some of the way. There's no way I can keep up with you lot."

Gregory dropped to all fours, stretching and limbering up for the run. "Gran and Greenborrow spoke the truth. Anything less would be an insult."

"Well, you're going to like the next part then, too. There are teams of humans with the prototype weapons all along the trail. To make things more interesting, Greenborrow ward-spelled some of their scopes as well. So don't assume the human teams won't be able to see past your shadow magic."

"This hunt shall be fun," Gregory rumbled happily.

Anna snorted. "If the enemy teams pinpoint our location, we have to try to neutralize the threat with nonlethal force before they tag us. Close combat will be hand to hand."

"They aren't using real bullets, are they?" Lillian asked, although her voice didn't sound concerned, more curious.

"Of course not." Anna paused again, her eyes tracking back to Gregory and then away to take in Shadowlight. "Nonlethal. No killing. No maiming. Understood?"

Gregory knew this, of course, but nodded agreement

for Shadowlight's benefit. The younger gargoyle was nearly vibrating with adrenaline.

"If all goes well with the newly warded prototype rifles, we'll do further tests in the coming days."

Again, Gregory nodded agreement. "Although this day is about more than testing the military's new toys."

With a huff of amusement, he waved at the three of them. "This is also a cub training session. The pooka has agreed to help train you."

Having heard his name, the black pony darted between two trees and into view for a moment before vanishing back into the shadows.

"Magic," Anna grunted sourly but merely folded her arms under her breasts. Lillian, on the other hand, looked somewhat eager.

"Once you have mastered shadow magic, your enemies will find you a difficult target to eradicate." Gregory reached out and plucked a bit of lacy shadow where it had been cast upon the ground by the thick tree canopy high above. "Shadows can do far more than hide you from your enemies' eyes."

He indicated the seemingly harmless bit of shadow resting in his open palm and then shaped it into sharp little obsidian shards and flung them one at a time toward a tree trunk ten feet away.

The shadow shards found their mark and bit deep into the tree's trunk, some sending pieces of bark flying.

Anna whistled low in her throat. "Totally badass. Didn't know you could do that."

Gregory's ears flicked in her direction. "You will be able

to do so as well, once trained. Although, I'm not sure if you're far enough into your development to summon shadows yet. That's what I hope to learn today."

"Fun times." Anna's tone was humorous, but he scented her unease.

He couldn't blame the human. She'd had a lot dumped on her in the last few days. Anna was doing admirably, considering.

"Like moonlight," he continued to explain, "All shadows possess an innate bit of magic. With practice, you can make that magic resonate to your call, shaping it to your will. Once you've mastered that, you can feed your own magical strength into it, turning it into a far more deadly force."

Shadowlight yawned, his earlier enthusiasm clearly waning. "But I already know all this. Can I go hunt with the pooka while you teach Lillian and Anna the beginnings?"

"Not so fast young one. All gargoyles are born with the knowledge of shadow magic, but it takes much practice to truly master it. Knowledge and experience are two very different things. One day your life may depend on your mastery of both."

With a flick of his wrist and a simple mental command, ropes of shadows erupted from the ground at Shadow-light's feet and coiled around his body. Before the younger gargoyle could summon his own magic to fight back, Gregory released him.

"You see?"

Shadowlight's ears pinned to the sides of his head in

embarrassment, but he nodded. "Yes. I want to be able to do that. Show me."

"And so, I shall."

It took the better part of two hours. When Gregory deemed them proficient in the most basic forms of shadow magic, he led them out into the forest to go play with the humans.

CHAPTER FOURTEEN

nna silently led the way through the darkening forest. Throughout the day, Lillian and Shadow-light had alternated with her to take point. Gregory always stayed a bit behind to study them and force them to lead and adapt instead of relying on him.

As they navigated their way through the simulated warzone, Anna calculated that they had to be in the home stretch. It just depended on how many more enemy teams they encountered. Four hours of stomping through the bug-infested forest or bumping around on a gargoyle's back was enough even for Anna. Surprisingly, once they'd started the hunt, as the gargoyles insisted on calling it, Lillian was as enthusiastic as the males.

Anna was presently leading their small group on foot since her poor tortured body couldn't take anymore riding gargoyle-back at the moment. But even the gargoyles seemed thankful for the slower pace.

They'd managed to avoid detection for the most part. The two units who had detected them earlier in the day were swiftly neutralized by shadow magic. Anna secretly admitted she was pleased with her team's performance.

The first team of soldiers had found themselves ensnared by ropes of Shadowlight's magic that held them immobile until well after Anna's group was long past. The second time they encountered a team of soldiers, a mass of tree roots had boiled up out of the ground and tripped up the soldiers. Later, Lillian had shrugged and said she had meant to summon shadows, but the tree roots had worked well enough.

As for herself, Anna learned she was capable of commanding shadow. She wasn't sure if she should be elated or dismayed by her innate ability to summon the magic.

Still, it was a handy skill to have on a battlefield. Unfortunately, she was not at all certain she wanted to report all that she'd seen and learned in the short day.

Anna frowned at the bits of sky she could see through the tree canopy. By the light, and the lengthening shadows, the sun was already descending toward the horizon. Weariness was starting to encroach upon her consciousness.

Even the ever-energetic Shadowlight was showing signs of exhaustion. All in all, Anna was somewhat proud of her own performance. She had her teachers to thank for what she'd learned.

She glanced at the pooka. Yes, he was a yellow-eyed, evil-tempered little pony, but she couldn't fault him for his skills as a teacher or a tracker. He spotted and corrected their every little mistake. The black-hearted little bastard would make Drill Sargent Chambers proud.

Gregory was no less alert. Or soft. Together they played bad cop and bad cop very well.

"Halt," Gregory ordered.

Her training kicking in, she froze like she'd stepped on a mine. A large hand grabbed her arm and yanked her back.

A foot in front of her face a tree trunk exploded in a rain of bark and shredded wood fragments. The sound of rifle fire screamed through the forest.

"Live fire," she screamed at the top of her lungs. What the fuck were they doing with live rounds?

Anna dove for the ground.

For less than a heartbeat, she thought it might have been a mistake. Then the forest erupted a second time. That was no mistake.

She cursed the fact she didn't have any weapons. But it was a training session. She wasn't supposed to need firearms. She didn't even have her Browning, but she did have something else.

All around her the shadows began to reverberate.

The pooka was faster. He darted past her location, heading for the origin of the rifle fire. His black legs a blur, he raced full tilt toward the unseen enemy, only to veer to the left seconds later. He vanished behind a thicket with a neighed challenge.

Human screams rang out and then fell silent.

Anna scrambled for better cover and ducked down behind the massive trunk of an oak as more bullets streaked through the air where she'd just been crouching.

Somewhere behind her a gargoyle grunted in pain, followed by a second deep snarl of rage.

"Shadowlight?" Anna kept her voice quiet and controlled, but fear for the youngling was pounding through her blood.

A second glance behind showed her that Gregory was the one who had roared in rage. He stood over Lillian. A vortex of shadows spun around him, protecting his mate from further damage.

Anna could smell blood though, so some bullets had found flesh. A grenade detonated far too close. Dirt and leaf litter pelted her and then she could smell nothing but the stink of propellant.

Her eyes watering, she searched desperately for the kid.

Guided by an instinct that always seemed to know where the young gargoyle was, she found him belly down on the ground a little less than twenty feet away. He was conscious. Thank God. But that was all she could ascertain from her position. Unfortunately, he looked like he was going to get up and attack.

"Don't move," Anna growled at him. "I'll come to you."

She summoned more shadows to form a shield. Not knowing if her command of magic was anywhere near great enough to stop bullets, she stayed low to the ground. Even so, she felt when a bullet ripped through her pack.

That was too damned close. So much for magical mastery of the shadows.

Two other things became apparent as she crawled toward Shadowlight's position. Either she'd allowed her new magic to slip and expose her location, or whoever the fuck was shooting at her had somehow gotten their hands on the prototype weapons. She preferred scenario one over scenario two.

The next unsettling realization was that if Gregory hadn't grabbed and hauled her back, it would have been her head, not a tree, which blew apart all over the forest floor.

Her blood still rushing with adrenaline, she forced herself to move slowly so as not to disturb the undergrowth around her.

Even if the enemy couldn't see them, shaking underbrush would give away her position just as readily.

The crawl to Shadowlight's location felt like a lifetime, but she finally made it to his position. Miraculously, he'd stayed put as she'd ordered, and no more bullets were presently whizzing overhead.

Which probably meant the unknown enemy was on the move.

Over the stink of hot metal and propellant, her newly heightened gargoyle senses picked up the scent of more humans. Males. At least seven different men by the sweat scent carried on the breeze. Her ears strained to catch some sound, but they were still ringing painfully from the sharp report of the rifle fire.

She crawled the last few feet to Shadowlight. The scent of blood was stronger now, and the gargoyle's scent was tainted with pain. Her stomach tightened with horror and fear.

"How bad are you hurt?"

Shadowlight was watching the forest in the direction the gunfire had come, but he flicked an ear in her direction, listening. "They managed to get my right wing. The membrane, not the bone."

The gargoyle bowed his head and turned his gaze upon her. His nostrils flared as he dragged in a deep breath. "Are you hurt?"

His question echoed hers, but she heard a quiver in his voice.

"I'm good."

He whined softly. "You're sure?"

"Don't you worry, I'm a tough bitch to kill."

"But they came so close. If Gregory hadn't..." His voice broke.

Damn. The poor kid. First, he lost his father. Then his mother was nearly killed and remained in a coma. Now some asshole had shot him and just about removed Anna's head from her shoulders right in front of the kid. Shadowlight thought she was going to die and leave him, too.

Rage replaced fear. Whoever the fuck was responsible was going to pay for terrifying the young gargoyle.

"You stay close to me, and I'll get us out of here," Anna said. *And then I'm coming back to hunt some heartless, spineless bastards who willingly fired upon an eight-year-old child.* It didn't matter that he was a gargoyle.

She glanced around. Now that she knew Shadowlight wasn't mortally wounded, she again looked for the others.

Anna found Gregory first. His massive form was still shielding Lillian from her view. The male wasn't just sheltering his girlfriend though. He was still summoning wave after wave of deadly shadow magic.

With a guttural word, the first wave of power raced forward, hunting their enemies.

In less than ten seconds there was an agonized scream. The second for the night. By the sound, this victim was at least sixty feet away, off somewhere to the right of the game trail.

A second and third pained shout rang out as more of Gregory's magic found its mark.

Hmmm. Maybe Anna wouldn't have to lead Shadowlight away to safety. Gregory was doing an excellent job of rendering the present location safe.

A fifth soldier broke cover and ran, apparently trying to fall back to a safer location.

But there was nowhere safe for this soldier to run. The pooka raced out from behind his thicket in pursuit of the human. He darted between two trees and shouldered the fleeing human hard enough to send him flying. Anna's attention snapped to another flash of motion as a sixth soldier rose up out of the cover and took aim at the pooka.

With a snarl, Shadowlight bolted for the soldier. More of Gregory's magic was already in pursuit, so Anna scanned the immediate area looking for dead man number seven.

Two seconds later she spotted him raising his rifle's muzzle toward Shadowlight. Darkness descended upon Anna. Rage. Fear. The need to protect. The need to destroy. They all warred within her until her mind clicked to the realization that destruction would sate all the other needs.

Kill the enemy and Shadowlight would be safe.

She rose up from her hiding place and darted forward

with superhuman speed. As she ran, she dropped her shielding spell that hid her from view.

She wanted the enemy's attention, needed it upon her, not the child. She roared, a deep snarling sound that shouldn't have come from a human chest. Anna darted across the distance, weaving around trees and leaping over fallen trunks and anything else in her path.

The soldier realized she was closing in on him. The muzzle of his gun started to swing toward her. But he was too slow.

Before her target could level his rifle at her, she slapped it out of the way and continued forward, her speed and momentum driving the bigger soldier back. She rode him to the ground and sank her new talons into his wrists, digging deep until he released the rifle with a scream.

He grabbed at a sidearm, but she blocked him, and then tore the gun free and tossed it away. When he reached for his knife, she snarled a deep inhuman sound. His arm snapped like a twig in her grasp.

The man howled in pain, but she wasn't finished yet. She grabbed up the rifle and brought it down. His good arm managed to block the first blow, but she smacked it out of the way.

"You tried to kill the kid. Only monsters kill children." She screamed at him as the rage drove her to a greater need for violence. She brought the rifle's butt against the human's head again and again. Blood splattered her in a fine spray.

She'd broken his nose and likely a cheekbone, but the bastard was still breathing.

"He's just a child," she screamed and raised the rifle high above her head.

"Anna, no." Shadowlight's voice was young sounding and pain-filled, but his will was strong and reached deep into her mind. "You will stop now."

As if his words were a command, she released the rifle. It thumped to the ground beside the unconscious soldier underneath her.

The soldier was nearly unrecognizable.

She'd beaten him bloody.

She shook her head to clear it but still nothing made sense. No that wasn't true. Something made sense in the madness. Shadowlight's familiar voice.

What the hell was wrong with her?

"Come away now," Shadowlight urged. "The threat is past."

Anna came to her feet, obedient to Shadowlight's command.

But it was Gregory who finally approached and urged her away from the human at her feet.

"Shadowlight is right. Come." Gregory reached out and took her arm. At his touch, the red fog blanketing her mind seemed to lift.

She shook her head again. "What? What's wrong with me?"

Shadowlight trotted up on her opposite side and bumped his muzzle under her hand. "The humans have been defeated. You can relax now."

"Listen to Shadowlight and come away," Gregory said. "We'll get to the bottom of this later. First, we need to see to Lillian and Shadowlight's injuries. Are you in control of yourself?"

It was a simple question. One that should have an easy answer. But the answer was evasive.

Was she in control of herself?

It didn't feel like it.

But she nodded, and Gregory stepped away from her to see to Lillian. When she looked back to Shadowlight, it was to see that he'd reared up to stand on two legs. Anna immediately noticed his shell-shocked look.

She turned and then enfolded him in a bear hug. "I'm sorry, kid."

Shadowlight returned her fierce hug

"Why did they try to kill us? I thought they were allies."

"I'm not sure, hon." *But I'm damned well going to find out.*

When Shadowlight released her at last, she glanced around to check on Lillian and Gregory again but noticed the black pony rolling on his back and grunting. Had he been injured? If it didn't mean leaving the kid unguarded or exposing him to new horror, she would have gone and checked on the Fae they simply called Pooka.

Gregory barked out something sharp and inhuman at the Fae. After a moment the pooka levered himself back to all fours with another grunt and then gave himself a good shake. Only then did he trot over toward the Avatars.

"Oh, God. Did he...? Gods, that's so nasty. I think I'm going to puke," Lillian said. She was still in gargoyle form at the moment, but if she'd been a dryad, Anna would have bet the other woman would be a bit green.

Anna scanned the pooka, trying to see what distressed Lillian so much. That's when she noticed the pooka's black pelt shone damply. And now that he was closer, her gargoyle senses could detect the dense coppery odor of blood. Lots of blood.

"What the hell?"

Shadowlight bumped his muzzle against her shoulder to get her attention. "Pookas roll in the blood of their fallen enemies after battle."

Then the cub flicked a mildly horrified looked down Anna's own blood smeared body. "I didn't realize humans did the same."

Anna glanced down at her bloodstained uniform.

How was she ever going to explain this mess to her superiors? And for that matter, how were her superiors going to smooth over the massive rift this attack would cause. Anna had a few other questions all vying for attention, too.

Top of the list was finding out who the soldiers that had attacked them were. Why did they attack? Who did they work for? The questions went on and on. But whatever the answers, the motive was clear. The realization that humans weren't the only sentient species on the planet was bound to put a bee up the ass of every elitist and human-centric crazy this side of the equator.

With a deeply unhappy sigh, Anna watched as Gregory dragged the soldiers to one location.

Anna needed to answer Shadowlight's earlier question and hopefully quell his fear, even if it put her own differences in an uncomfortably bright light. "Humans don't generally make a habit of glorying in our killing. Certainly no rolling in an enemy's blood. I overreacted."

"I was in danger," Shadowlight said in a whisper. "You acted the way you did because of me. Because of what my blood has done to you. I'm sorry."

"I don't know what you're talking about. But don't worry, kid. I'm an adult and can deal with my own shit," Anna said and stroked another unruly lock of hair behind his ear. In truth, she knew what he was talking about, and she knew his words were true. But she didn't care. She would have protected him even without the blood's influence. "I need to go clean up and report this mess."

"I think your superiors already know," Gregory said as he stepped up to them. "I hear helicopters coming."

The other gargoyle had Lillian tucked against his side protectively. That's when Anna saw blood seeping down Lillian's arm from a graze. Other than that minor wound, the female gargoyle didn't seem to be harmed. She was in fact, alert and studying Anna.

"You might want to regain some...composure," Lillian said and paused as she flailed for a better word. In the end, she just rushed to the truth. "You look more gargoyle than you did before."

To reinforce her words, Lillian reached up and gestured at her own horns.

Anna felt her jaw drop. Oh, for fuck's sake. No. Nope. Can't be.

But when she reached up, she felt the wide bases of two horns. Yup. She had big-ass horns.

Shadowlight reached out and touched first one horn

and then the other. There was a mild heat in both horns, and then suddenly they were gone. Instantly her head felt lighter. How the hell hadn't she known about the horns earlier?

Well, that was one thing fixed. What other surprises awaited her? Dragging in a deep breath, Anna glanced down at her body. She took stock of her condition and was pleased to see she hadn't sustained any wounds or other disconcerting changes.

At least the horns were one less thing she'd have to explain in a report. She thought about asking Shadowlight how he had made them vanish, but at that moment she was too tired to care. She was just glad they were gone. She had enough weird-ass anomalies as it was.

Overhead a helicopter circled, its spotlight illuminating the area. In the distance, she could hear other vehicles approaching. Light armored vehicles by the sounds of the engines.

Great. She was in for a long night of debriefing and would later have scientists breathing down her neck.

"Do you wish to go elsewhere? We can." Shadowlight said, proving she still hadn't mastered the art of shielding her thoughts from the others.

Anna barked out a humorous laugh. "You know I do. But after Gran sees to the wound on your wing, I'll stay and answer every question my superiors have and maybe later after it's over, they'll let us rest for a bit."

The vehicles were still approaching fast, perhaps only two minutes out, when the unicorn galloped into the clearing. The Mother's Sorceress was astride his back, and

Daryna was living up to her name. Raw, white, sizzling power danced along her skin and silhouetted her against the lengthening shadows of dusk.

"Well. This doesn't look good." Anna stepped between Daryna and the gargoyle child.

Daryna paid them no mind. Her attention was focused on the seven-man team where Gregory had dragged them all together in one pile. Anna was surprised to see that none of them were dead. Yet. But they had an assortment of wounds. Some grievous, others shallow. But all seven soldiers were bloodied and would have a long recovery.

Though by the look of them, Anna wasn't certain if all would survive. The man she'd beaten and the two the pooka had taken down were the worst. Their futures looked the most uncertain.

While she might not shed a tear over what happened to them in the heat of battle, it did not mean she would sit back and do nothing while the soldiers were murdered in cold blood. Hell, they were soundly defeated and were presently unconscious.

Daryna dismounted from the unicorn and then stalked up to the fallen soldiers. She spread her arms wide and held her palms up, globes of blazing magic at the ready to rain fire and death down upon the soldiers.

CHAPTER FIFTEEN

*D*aryna's sudden arrival surprised Lillian, but it also jarred her out of the numbing shock that had started to creep across her being. Daryna's intent was obvious. And while Lillian wasn't feeling precisely sympathetic to the soldiers, she couldn't just stand back and watch them be snuffed from existence. Anna must have been thinking the same thing for she left Shadowlight to step between Daryna and the fallen soldiers.

Swiftly stepping out and away from Gregory's sheltering wing, Lillian darted forward and circled around to stand beside Corporal Mackenzie.

"Lillian, step aside." Daryna's words were brisk and dripping with command.

"Nope."

One of Daryna's eyebrows arched up, showing her surprise. "These traitors must be put down, or their fear and hate will only spread like a disease."

"That's not your call to make," Anna barked out, the rifle she'd taken from Shadowlight at the ready.

Behind Lillian, a growl broke the silence. Gregory. Really not happy. Lillian turned and pointed a finger at her mate. "You stay out of this."

Gregory huffed out a startled grunt but swallowed back his aggression. Her gargoyle protector brought into line for a moment, she turned her attention toward Daryna. "You! Stow the fire and brimstone act. Violence generally only begets more violence. We need cooler heads. Yes, they attacked us. Yes, we used force to subdue them. But they are helpless now and are no threat to us. Their punishment will be decided by the humans. Not us."

"Move out of the way."

"Not until you're rational." Lillian spread her arms and wings wide, palms held out empty. "I'm not going to let you kill unconscious men. And I highly doubt you're going to attack me just to get to them."

Mind you, she expected Daryna knew a few spells and could get around Lillian's defenses without much trouble.

Gregory, who had been stalking around the three women, finally released a chuckle. The tension in the air lessened a hundredfold. He paced over to Lillian and nuzzled at her hand.

A foolish thrill of happiness warmed her heart. Gregory had sided with her over his sorceress.

"I think the three of you must be some of the most formidable females to be found in any of the realms. I suppose it's good that I adore strong women." Gregory stood and wrapped a wing around Lillian, urging her up against his side. Then he reached out and wound his tail around Daryna, forcing her to lower her arm. When Daryna didn't extinguish her magic, Gregory dragged her over to him.

Daryna hissed something but swallowed back her power before it could touch Gregory's skin.

"There will be no more death this night. Besides, surely the future will hold enough. Lillian is correct. These humans will be turned over to their superiors." Gregory glowered at them.

"They must be punished," Daryna said, sounding taken aback.

"And they will," Gregory said in a soothing voice. "As much as I would like to deal with them myself, our human allies will need to make the next move. If I do not like what that move is, we will discuss alternatives."

Lillian side-eyed Gregory. "Thanks for the support. I think."

Still, some of Lillian's weariness fell away, and she felt another wave of warmth that Gregory had sided with her over his sorceress.

Daryna sighed, the tense set of her shoulders relaxed. "You have more experience with these humans. I will bow to your wisdom in this, my protector."

Lillian was certain there was a silent 'this time' at the end of Daryna's sentence. But for now, she'd settle for temporary peace. She drew a deep breath and let it hiss out between her lips. "Good. Because I'm sweaty, smelly, sore and bleeding again."

Inspecting the graze on her arm, she noted it still stung

and seeped blood readily. "And I'm also hungry, and I want to shower. So let's keep the damn peace when these nice soldiers all come rolling up."

She nodded at the first of several armored vehicles sliding to a halt. Apparently, they were closer to finishing the fifty-kilometer run than she'd thought if the vehicles had already made their way to them so swiftly.

"Oh, for fuck's sake. They brought scientists with them." Anna groaned and dropped her head into her hands.

Shadowlight paced beside Anna. His tail flicked happily. "I like the scientists. They're nice."

Anna just shook her head. "You only like them because they give you candy."

"Do not."

"Ha. Yes, you do. That reminds me. We should have the talk about not taking candy from strangers."

"But I like candy," he admitted.

When Shadowlight leaned against Anna's leg, she reached out and patted the young gargoyle on the shoulder. "Come on. We'll deal with this and then see if we can find something sweet and totally bad for us. I think we deserve it after all this."

Lillian watched as the unlikely duo walked to meet the soldiers filing out of the vehicles. Even though she was tired, dirty and sore, a smile pulled back her lips, flashing fangs in a toothy gargoyle grin.

The three realms might just have a grumpy soldier and an exuberant gargoyle child to thank for a peace treaty which could save them all.

Though, they couldn't do it alone. Lillian glanced up at Gregory and then over to his other side where Daryna stood looking at the approaching humans with disdain and anger.

Sighing, Lillian squared her shoulders. "Come on. The sooner we get this over with, the sooner we can get cleaned up and find some food. It's been a hellishly long day."

CHAPTER SIXTEEN

After the epic disaster of the first joint training exercise with the humans, Lillian returned to their quarters with Gregory and Daryna while Gran, Whitethorn, and the banshee remained with the humans to salvage the peace treaty and see to Shadowlight and Anna's wounds.

At the moment, Lillian doubted if Gregory was feeling particularly forgiving. Actually, his dark expression hinted that he was probably trying to figure out a way to deal with the Battle Goddess without the help of the humans.

"Oh, come on," Lillian said as they trudged up the stairs and turned down the hall that led to their chambers. "The day could have turned out far worse. No one has died yet."

"You sound much calmer. You realize you weren't half so calm when you thought Shadowlight had been harmed."

"So what? I embrace double standards. If they'd hurt

Shadowlight, you would've had to fight me for the kill." Lillian sighed, her humor vanishing. "This incident was brought about by less than a dozen humans. We couldn't just punish all of them for the acts of a few."

"Innocent? If Resnick and the rest of his kind had been doing their duty, they should have scented the deception on the soldiers under their command."

"You forget humans don't have the highly developed senses of a gargoyle." Once inside her rooms, Lillian started to peel off her bloodstained clothing. "Even we didn't catch the dark intent of the traitors until we were practically on top of them. How can you blame all the humans for the failings of a few?"

Gregory huffed again, wanting to deny her words, but he couldn't.

Lillian pulled her crusted hair away from the graze on her shoulder and growled out a pained hiss.

"I should have braided this mess." She pulled her thick mane over her shoulder and studied the wound more carefully. "The graze burns like a sonofabitch."

"Let Gregory clean the wound," Daryna said as she stepped closer to examine it. "Then I'll heal it."

"Sure." Lillian glanced at Daryna, not really wanting the other woman to use her magic on the wound, but it wasn't like Lillian could say no without raising suspicions. And that was the last thing she needed this night. The banshee's concerns were still prominent in her mind. Focusing on the small wound, she pushed her other concerns away to deal with later as she probed at the minor injury.

"There doesn't seem to be dirt or foreign debris in it. It's all yours," she said with a glance in Gregory's direction.

He didn't get the first aid kit like a human would. Instead, he stepped closer and dipped his muzzle down to the wound. At the first swipe of his tongue, Lillian grunted even though she expected it.

Not that she should have been surprised. Gargoyles were touchy-feely and weren't turned off by a bit of blood. He continued to lap at the wound for a couple more minutes and then nuzzled his way up her shoulder to the curve of her neck.

His warm, male scent wrapped around her like a comforting blanket. Having Gregory close was pleasant. She dragged in a deeper lungful of his scent. Her thoughts turned to more intimate things than the wound on her forearm.

At least until a movement behind Gregory caught her attention. Her gaze focused on Daryna and that effectively smothered the embers of desire Gregory's presence had been fanning.

Yep. Nope.

No audience.

Lillian stepped away from Gregory and then presented her wounded arm to Daryna.

"You were going to heal it. I think it's clean enough." Truthfully, the small sting had already vanished. Gargoyle saliva had a healing compound or enzyme in it that made quick work of wounds.

Daryna stepped closer and touched Lillian's arm, lightly drawing a fingertip along the abrasion. Just one swipe, a bit of tingling heat, and the wound was nothing more than a pale line against her obsidian skin.

Lillian huffed in acknowledgment and then realized she was turning as nonverbal as Gregory. "Thank you, Daryna."

The Sorceress nodded her head. "If you will allow me..." Her gaze dropped down to the barely noticeable bump that curved Lillian's otherwise toned gargoyle form.

As a dryad, her pregnancy was more noticeable. But in her gargoyle form, not so much. Lillian decided that might come in handy when she was further along. Not to mention everything about her gargoyle form was bigger including her hips.

Again, Lillian felt the slight heat and tingle of Daryna's power as it hummed along her skin and sank into tissue and bone. After a moment, the other woman glanced up. "All is well with our little one."

"Good. And now I call dibs on the shower."

Lillian stepped around Daryna and Gregory and made for the bathroom. Had Daryna not been present, Lillian would have invited Gregory, but as it was now, she wasn't certain if he'd be the only one to join her.

Fate had an evil sense of humor. She and Gregory had finally found a way to be together, and then Daryna had used magic to will herself into existence.

My life sucks, Lillian decided as she entered the bathroom. Once inside, she summoned her magic and returned to dryad form. At least shape shifting was becoming easier. Turning to the mirror, she examined the small white scar.

The pale mark reminded her of Daryna. With a sour

expression at her reflection, she turned and shed what passed for clothing in her gargoyle form.

Cranking the hot water to steaming, she stepped under the pounding spray. Blood turned the water a pinkish color and dirt soon muddied it further. Unfortunately, her unease and jealousy couldn't be washed away so easily.

Gregory stared at the closed bathroom door, listening to the sounds of splashing water as Lillian washed up. Had the situation been different, he would've joined her. He was rather fond of showering with his mate. Memories of other times flashed to the forefront of his mind. He grinned.

"We should not place her in danger like that again." Daryna's voice was an exact match for Lillian's down to the tone, cadence, and timbre. It never failed to draw his attention.

He flicked an ear in her direction but continued to watch the bathroom door. "I didn't intend to place Lillian in danger—not that she has ever listened to me once she's set her mind to something. However, you are correct. What happened this day could have turned out much worse."

Gregory glanced down at his hands, his talons flexing. He forced himself to relax. Worrying about what might have been was not something that was ever beneficial. "Later, I will speak with Vivian and discuss having every last human that works directly or indirectly with the Fae scanned by myself or one of the others capable of sensing intention and deceit."

Daryna walked a semicircle around him, her glance flicking over his form. After another half turn, she stepped in closer. He relaxed when she only reached up and removed a twig from his mane. She smoothed his hair back down with her hand. "We cannot allow something like what occurred today to happen again. It was careless. And carelessness will get us killed in a war against the Lady of Battles."

"I was too busy playing at mentor. I shouldn't have allowed myself to become so distracted by that role that I forgot my true duty—to see to your and Lillian's protection."

Daryna laughed. "Don't, as Lillian would say, beat yourself up over this. I, too, underestimated the humans. It won't happen again."

She turned from him, walked over to the dresser, and then picked up one of the brushes Lillian often used on his mane. Daryna returned to his side and gestured for him to sit on the bed. He did but glanced toward the bathroom door again. Sounds of water still reached his ears, so he shrugged and allowed Daryna to start working on his mane, a job usually performed by Lillian.

It was just hair, he told himself. It was a harmless enough activity.

Daryna settled on the bed behind him, her knees on either side of his hips. He tensed, wondering if she would forget herself and touch him as she had last night. He did not wish to hurt her, but this thing between them wasn't what he'd always known.

However, nothing more than the brush of bristles touched him, so he relaxed and enjoyed the sensation of having his mane combed smooth. He rumbled a contented sigh and allowed his eyes to drift shut.

They snapped back open a moment later when Daryna hugged him from behind. Warm lips brushed the curve of his shoulder.

His wings twitched and unfurled, forcing her arms away from his body. They needed some new rules. Apparently, he hadn't been clear enough the night before.

"Lillian will be finished her shower soon..."

Daryna stood, and then stepped around in front of him and settled on his lap. "Well, then I better hurry if I want to enjoy the other half of my soul for a brief time."

Her hands brushed across his chest, stroking and kneading his tense muscles. When he opened his mouth to say something, she pressed kisses along his throat and worked her way down.

This close, her scent was stronger, familiar and just as addictive as Lillian's. Her magic raced over his skin a moment later, and he'd be lying to himself if he said he didn't like it. He'd missed his other half. He always did when they were born in separate bodies. The desire awakening in his blood was also familiar.

His sorceress pressed closer, brushing herself against him. Her left hand grasped one of his larger ones and guided it to her breast while the right settled on his hip where her thumb stroked back and forth slowly with promise.

Even as his body responded, his mind snapped into focus. Yes, she was the Mother's Sorceress, the other half of his soul. And, yes, he loved her—always would. But his heart only wanted Lillian's touch.

"No." Many times in the past when the loneliness became too great, they'd played love games—dangerous, delightful games that walked the line of what their sacred vows allowed.

This lifetime was different.

He captured her hands and brought them up to his chest, to rest over his beating heart. "This doesn't mean I love you less, but I will not partake of these types of games with you until you and Lillian are reunited in one body. It's not fair to either of you."

Daryna broke eye contact and looked down.

"I'm sorry," she mumbled softly. "I remembered what you said last night. Still, I can't just deny what my heart still remembers and craves. But neither will I force myself on you."

When she glanced back up, she slipped her right hand free of his grip—he let her—and then she cupped the side of his face. "But I would have one kiss from you each day all the same. That will be enough for me."

Gregory wasn't certain of the wisdom, but her request was reasonable. In the past, he'd never denied his lady anything that was in his power to grant. She was a part of him, and he couldn't bring himself to deny her a simple kiss.

"Get a room."

The words burned through the haze of confusion. Lillian stood in the bathroom door wearing a robe and toweling her hair dry. "And by get a room, I mean a different one."

CHAPTER SEVENTEEN

*L*illian had exited the bathroom about thirty seconds before. Plenty of time to see Daryna straddle Gregory's lap as they kissed and caressed each other. Lillian's heart had frozen in her chest, sympathizing with her shocked mind which didn't know what to do.

She'd stood there, silent, her heart breaking. It shouldn't have come as a surprise—she'd been expecting something like this since Daryna had first emerged from the tree. The Gargoyle Protector and the Mother's Sorceress had a long history—an ancient one. They'd loved each other longer than Lillian had been alive.

Hell, longer than the human civilization had been around.

So, it wasn't a surprise that they would share a deep affection and intimacy. Still, Lillian's mortal-raised heart ached, her throat tightening with unshed tears.

Then Gregory had told Daryna no.

A clear 'no' that left no room for misinterpretation. He had denied her. Lillian dragged in a deep breath. When she released it, much of the earlier heartache was expelled with it.

Gregory had denied his sorceress because he was loyal to Lillian.

Narrowing her eyes, she focused on the back of Daryna's head. The other two still weren't aware that she'd exited the bathroom. Lillian waited to see how the other woman took Gregory's rejection.

When Daryna reached up and caressed Gregory's cheek, pressing her courtship, Lillian felt her claws lengthening. The now familiar vision of her grabbing Daryna by the hair and dragging her from the room kicking and screaming formed in her mind.

However, Lillian held her position while Daryna apologized to Gregory for acting like a cat in heat.

Fisting her fingers, she forced her claws to return to their regular length. She listened to Daryna's crocodile tears and apologies to Gregory and then after a coy pause, the demand for a kiss. And how that would be enough to satisfy.

I call bullshit, Lillian thought to herself and then cleared her throat. "Get a room."

When she had Gregory's full, guilt-laced attention, she added, "And by get a room, I mean a different one."

Gregory bolted upright. Only a firm grip on Daryna's shoulder prevented her from sprawling on her ass.

Damn. That would have been entertaining. Lillian shoved

the petty notion aside. This new development needed to be dealt with, so none of them were distracted. They had a war to prepare for. The Lady of Battles would certainly enjoy it if her enemies were suddenly at each other's throats.

And Gregory looked so torn. Her beloved didn't know what to do, but clearly he thought he was guilty of something.

His look of anguish was enough to extinguish her petty thoughts. For his sake, she would find a way to work with Daryna.

"Lillian." He released Daryna once she had her balance and then he stepped away from her. "Forgive me. Both of you, forgive me. I should be strong enough to be the protector you both deserve. I should not allow my own needs and desires to taint my judgment."

"Gregory, I'm sorry," Lillian said.

He stepped further away from them both, toward the door. "I will not choose between you or hurt either of you. So, I shall be your protector, your loyal gargoyle, but not your beloved."

"Gregory, wait," Lillian called softly and held out a hand. "You have not failed us or betrayed us. Don't let this drive a wedge between us. That is what the Lady of Battles would enjoy the most if she knew."

When Gregory didn't come to her immediately, she went to him and grasped one of his hands in hers. He didn't try to pull away, so she gestured Daryna over as well.

Daryna watched Lillian with what could only be described as surprise, touched with a hint of admiration.

"Yeah. I promise I won't start any slap downs or bitch fights."

Again, Daryna's eyes widened. And then to Lillian's surprise, the other woman started to laugh. "Perhaps another time? Gregory might enjoy the show."

Lillian grunted, but felt a begrudging twitch of her lips at Daryna's words.

She turned her attention entirely upon Gregory. And tapped him on the chest. "I came in time to see you say no to Daryna. And I thank you for being honorable. But I am not so selfish to deny you the other half of your soul. Or to deny Daryna hers."

"Lillian, I—"

She cut him off. "I don't really want to share your affections. Not even with myself, as it were, but we all need each other to be strong and whole. No secrets and no deceptions. And Gregory, that's why I won't make you choose."

She reached out and turned his face until his eyes met hers. "However, just in case you get confused, if you want more than to kiss," she ran her hands over her curves. "This is the body for that. We don't need any accidental demigods suddenly being born into the Mortal Realm. We have enough trouble."

Daryna made a soft noise. It almost sounded like a gasp. Had she just managed to surprise an immortal sorceress?

By the time Lillian looked up, Daryna's expression was as stoic as always. *Hmmm. Damn. Must've imagined it,* Lillian thought a bit sourly. She'd have liked to shock the age-old sorceress out of her calm demeanor for once.

Daryna wasn't going to humor her today it seemed.

"Lillian. Gregory. I, too, must ask forgiveness. I'm certainly old enough to know better than to wish for things I can never have. But that also means I'm old enough to know what a rare gift fate has given us in this lifetime." She stared at Lillian. "Don't waste the opportunity to be with the one we have always loved. And there is no need to be jealous for what Gregory still feels for me. I am but a memory. You are the Mother's Sorceress as the Divine Ones intended for this lifetime."

Daryna gave Lillian a little bow and then straightened and walked toward the door. "Gran said that she, the Fae council and the human military were likely to talk long into the night and that my presence would be appreciated when I'm able to join them."

Duty, Lillian thought sourly. "We should be there too."

It was the last place she wanted to go.

"No need. I will report everything I learn after the meeting is over. If other humans mean to harm us, I will find them, but you have my word I will leave any traitors for the human authorities to deal with."

"Are you sure?" Lillian didn't like the thought of shirking her duties.

"Yes. You and Gregory have both been tromping around the forest all day. You need rest worse than I do."

Daryna smiled serenely, and suddenly Lillian was in the other woman's thoughts.

"Our beloved needs soothing this night. He has been divided

and uncertain how to provide what we both need without hurting the other. Show him that he has been overthinking things. And, Lillian, if you can accept that Gregory's love is not limited, that he can, in fact, love us both without conflict, then that will make things easier for you." Daryna fell silent in Lillian's mind, but she could still feel the other's presence so wasn't surprised when she added one final thing.

"And if you can accept those truths, know that I will never attempt to seduce Gregory for more than a kiss every now and again."

Lillian arched an eyebrow. *"Agreed. And if you never try to take more than a kiss, I will never have to drag you out by your hair."*

Daryna was halfway to the door when her laughter rang out. *"Deal, my firstborn body."*

CHAPTER EIGHTEEN

Commander Gryton paced around the perimeter of the natural cavern that was now his temporary home. As far as such abodes went, he'd been in worse places while he went about his duties assigned by the Battle Goddess.

So far, the Mother's Sorceress—it was too strange to call or think of her as his mother yet—had been honest, teaching him things about controlling his magic that he'd never known.

And Daryna was fair in her teachings, never unduly harsh with her words or training techniques when he failed to grasp some concept. Unlike the Battle Goddess, who believed weakness and failure could be beaten or tortured out of a person.

Was this kindness and patience really what it was like to have a mother, he wondered? Or was this just another type of manipulation?

Because, really, she could simply be a far more accomplished liar than he gave her credit for.

Although…he'd been in her head during the training sessions and those times her memories and motives were open for him while she taught him about controlling and harnessing his vast and terrible fire magic. Nothing in her thoughts had hinted at a later betrayal.

Before she captured him, his power had been cascading out of his control. Had she not seized him and drained much of his wild power and started the process to teach him, he doubted he'd still be here. At least not as he was now.

His inability to control his own magic might have ended with this realm gaining a second sun. While the idea of a second sun to dance in binary sync with the star that already powered this solar system might be an interesting one, it wasn't how he wanted his present existence to end.

"That's why I am glad my hamadryad recognized you as our son. Otherwise, I might have lost you before I even had a chance to know you."

Daryna's voice appeared in the air, echoing from another location. Then with a slight buzz of power along his skin, she stepped through a portal and was standing at his side.

He'd grown accustomed to her sudden appearances and disappearances, as well as the seeming ease with which she read his mind. "Greetings, Sorceress."

She flashed him a smile, the warmth in it real and frighteningly addictive.

"Hello, my son."

She came and sat by the small fire he'd built earlier. Not that he needed one. Being a fire elemental, he could simply summon fire and make it burn without needing fuel. Although, there was something comforting about the smell of wood smoke.

It wasn't lost on Gryton that he could learn so much more than he already knew from this woman.

If he was willing to trust her completely.

So far, she'd done nothing to betray him. As a result, he was prone to letting his guard down around her far more than he should. "Did you achieve what you had hoped?"

"I must admit, my day wasn't very productive. There was an incident with the humans. A minor betrayal. But it was enough to set back the alliance." She sighed and flicked her hair over her shoulder in annoyance. "Every moment we are pulled away from our rightful task to fix some little insignificant issue, we are drawn away from our preparations for the war with the Battle Goddess."

"Well, at least my day wasn't a complete waste," Gryton began. "I was able to do more scouting around the military camp earlier this evening as well as in the stone cottage that's serving as a meeting place for the Fae."

Gryton turned the rabbit cooking over the coals. Belatedly he glanced between his simple meal and the female who had given him life. "Are you hungry? Rabbit is all I can offer. But you are welcome to share."

"No, but thank you." Daryna dropped a pack next to a ridge of rock that doubled as a bench. "I brought you some supplies. There's some food stolen from Vivian's hearth."

His interest piqued at the mention of the old witch's

cooking. Even cold, day-old food created by her hand was better than what he'd eaten back in the Battle Goddess's domain. He expected it was enchanted, but he didn't care.

Once all was said and done, and they defeated the Battle Goddess, he decided that if the old witch who was only known as Gran survived, he'd make sure she had a place in the new world.

"At least you were able to do some scouting."

Gryton glanced up at her. "The other Fae were not able to see me. Not even the gargoyle child and his pet berserker."

Daryna smiled. "You noticed that about the human hybrid as well."

He huffed in remembrance, his eyes narrowing. "I still have a scar from her. I would like to return the favor sometime."

She arched an eyebrow. "From what I saw in Lillian's memories, you already did."

"Her burns healed without even a scar to show for it," he pointed out.

"The hybrid is not our enemy. Leave her alone for now." Daryna's expression turned thoughtful. "You've been able to scout the area and determine the best location to capture the young gargoyle?"

He frowned at the fire. "I tracked the young gargoyle for the better part of two days — at least when he wasn't in the company of your male half."

"My male half? It wouldn't kill you to call him your father."

Actually, if Gregory learned the truth, he just might kill

Gryton. Regardless of what his mother said, he knew better than to trust his spells and mind tricks to work on his sire. "From what I overheard, there will be more of the training exercises like the one today. That will be the best time to capture Shadowlight. The rest of the time there are too many guards around."

"I'll have to do something to distract Gregory for you." Daryna frowned in thought.

Gryton cleared his throat. "Separating the child from his berserker will be almost as difficult."

"Yes, Anna is like a mother to him now. Even if she wasn't being influenced by Shadowlight's altered biology, she would still be protective of the youngster. The need to protect seems to be hardwired into her DNA."

"Hardwired? DNA?" The Mother's Sorceress sometimes used words he didn't know. He hated feeling inferior.

"They are human words that simply speak of bloodlines and origins," she explained. After a moment her expression turned thoughtful again as she started to pace around the cavern. When she completed one revolution, she halted before him.

"That protective nature might be what we can use against her. If there is some new danger to the cub, her nature and training will demand she go find it and neutralize it before it can become a threat to Shadowlight."

Gryton arched an eyebrow. "What would be a big enough distraction to draw away Gregory, Lillian, and the hybrid? If they're chasing me, I can't very well snatch the child."

"No."

"And you can't risk revealing our alliance yet."

"Hmmm. No." Daryna agreed.

Gryton had two other assets he hadn't told her about yet. He supposed now was the time for a show of trust. "I have two assets that might be helpful in this endeavor. When I first arrived here and was scouting the area, I found the two Fae that the human military had captured. When they were unconscious, I took the opportunity to weave a few subtle spells that would enslave them to my will. I simply have to trigger the spell, and they will be mine to command."

"Ah. You mean the sidhe Whitethorn and the sprite Goswin?"

"Yes."

"Good. Use them."

"Even with their help, it won't be enough of a distraction."

"No." Suddenly she grinned. "But if you call for reinforcements from the Magic Realm, you can use them as a distraction to lure away Gregory and Anna and then you can snatch Shadowlight and take him to Lord Death's domain."

Gryton grunted. There were two parts of the plan he didn't care for. "Gregory has command of his full power again. He'll make short work of whoever comes to my aid."

Again, Daryna smiled at him. "And that will rid us of a few enemies while furthering our plans."

"You're wagering a lot of hope that Lord Death doesn't just kill the gargoyle cub outright."

"I know Lord Death. His one great regret is that he

acted too quickly in destroying his sister's consort. Now he is rather too cautious." Daryna gave the cooking rabbit a turn. Fat dripped into the fire, making it pop and hiss. "He will study the cub and find him a pure heart. He'll then train him into a proper gargoyle who will serve the Light. But more importantly, Death will realize just what game his sister is playing and the type of power she now uses. Creation is the domain of the Divine Ones, not for the likes of a mere servant."

"And you think Lord Death will not overlook his sister's breaking of divine will?"

"Yes."

Gryton refrained from commenting that his own existence was in violation of divine will. Instead, he said, "Do you actually think seeing what Shadowlight is will stir Lord Death to act faster? I'm not sure even that will be enough for him to risk breaking the duality curse."

Daryna nodded as she gave the rabbit another turn. "Maybe not. But we'll prod him with more evidence. Anna won't just sit by and do nothing. Eventually, her magic will drag her back to Shadowlight's side. Once Lord Death learns that his twin has found a way to create female gargoyles, he'll realize that his sister has achieved a way to breed a new army that will serve her. It will push him into acting."

One side of his mouth twitched as he fought a grin. "You figured that bit out about the female gargoyles already?"

"Yes. It was no great feat."

"The Battle Goddess said that once the gargoyles meet

their female counterparts, some will fall prey to baser instincts and will be easy enough to seduce into serving her instead." Gryton arched a brow. "Once Shadowlight was mature, she planned for him to convert her succubus demons into gargoyle hybrids. Those females can be very persuasive."

"It is good that River defected and took Shadowlight with her. I would have hated to face and kill my host's baby brother in battle."

She reached out and removed the rabbit from the fire. "Your dinner is ready and I must return soon."

Gryton nodded. "I will summon three of my least liked lieutenants to act as unwitting distractions for your other half to hunt down and destroy while I capture the gargoyle child."

"I will see that Gregory agrees to take part in another of those training exercises. It will take some soothing to get all parties working together again. Give me four days."

"You're sure?"

"Yes."

Gryton started to pull apart the rabbit, using his claws and fangs to tear into the stringy meat. Around a mouthful of food, he said, "Then three days from now before dawn colors the sky, I will make my way to the hamadryad and use her strength to project a message to my people. I'll share with them what I've learned about the Fae and military alliance and that there will be a training session the following day that will provide the perfect opportunity to snatch the young gargoyle."

"Good. After this, we will be one step closer to ridding ourselves of our enemy."

CHAPTER NINETEEN

Gregory stood off to one side as scientists fitted Anna and Shadowlight with more of their strange sensors and bits of technology.

"Oh, for fuck's sake," Anna growled. "Just give me the goddamn thing and I'll do it myself."

"Language!" Gran barked as she tapped her staff against the ground threateningly. "I won't have that kind of speech around the young one."

"I've heard worse." Shadowlight said then asked, "What's a clusterf—?"

"Where did you hear that, sweetheart?" Gran asked without breaking stride. "And you shouldn't use words like that."

His brows scrunched up in thought.

Gregory tapped into Lillian's memories to learn the meaning of the human term and winced.

"But Anna uses them," Shadowlight said with a stubborn hint of challenge in his tone.

A resounding thump sounded as Gran's staff smacked down on Anna's shoulder.

"Ouch! Crazy old witch!"

Another blow landed with superhuman speed. "Damn it!"

A third landed with more force.

"You've got to be effing kidding me!" Anna dropped into a crouch, realizing she needed to defend herself since Gran wasn't going to relent.

Gregory wondered how long it would take the stubborn hybrid to figure out that if she simply filtered her mouth...

Gran's staff weaved back and forth menacingly while Anna retreated.

"Fine. I surrender!" Then under her breath, "But you're still a crazy old witch."

"I heard that," Gran hissed.

"I did too," Shadowlight said and looked like he was about to pounce on the two women and join the fun.

"Enough!" The command was barked out by Resnick. "We are ready to start."

Gran and Anna both looked mortified. Shadowlight merely dropped to all fours and raced around the others excitedly.

Gregory decided four days of training wasn't enough to turn his new cubs into respectable warriors. Every day since that first disastrous training session, Gregory had taken Lillian, Anna, and Shadowlight out into the forest to teach them more about shadow magic.

Still, he was taking no chances with his cubs' safety this time. Before Resnick had sent his teams out into the forest to lay their ambushes, Gregory had scanned and scented each member of the hunting teams that would be testing the prototype weapons. He hadn't bothered to hide in shadows.

After they had gotten over their initial shock, Resnick's soldiers had conducted themselves well and had proved they could adapt to whatever strange situation they found themselves in. They seemed open-minded enough and willing to cooperate with their new allies.

This time, Daryna and Gran stayed behind to meet with the military and other civilian leaders to hash out some new terms. Gregory didn't care what was agreed upon as long as it didn't involve him working directly with some paper-carrying, silver-tongued human.

When he wasn't training his young gargoyles, he enjoyed the relative peace and quiet of working with the sidhe metalsmiths as they forged more ward-spelled swords and other weapons for the Fae.

Daryna glanced up at him. "Working with the humans was your idea."

"Actually, it was Lillian's."

"Yeah," she whispered from his other side. "I'm sorry about that. Had I known that we would be moving targets for them to practice their marksmanship on, I might have agreed with you."

Gregory mentally agreed but decided not to comment further. His grumpiness spoke for itself. They'd been training each day. And while the sessions were helping

Lillian, Anna, and Shadowlight master their shadow magic and learn to fight as a team, it was also taking him from his other tasks. He missed not having other gargoyles to help with preparing for battle. Darkness had been a great aid for the short while he'd been with them. However, if other gargoyles came, he somehow doubted they'd come as friends. He still feared how the Lord of the Underworld would view Lillian, and now Shadowlight and Anna as well.

One problem at a time. Get the humans prepared. Then he'd do what he could to finish preparing the Fae of this world. Only then, once he'd done all he could for the earth, would he return to Lord Death and rally the Gargoyle Legion. He'd left that as the last task on his list for he feared the Lord of the Underworld might send him back to face the Divine Ones' judgment.

He'd reassured Lillian more than once that if the Divine Ones were truly angry at them for bending a few sacred laws and begetting a child, he and Lillian would already have been wiped from existence and recalled to the Spirit Realm immediately.

While his words might be true, it didn't mean there would be no punishment. He just hoped the punishment wouldn't result in his and Lillian's separation.

"What's wrong my gargoyle?" Daryna asked, her voice rich with concern for him.

He'd never been good at hiding his thoughts from her. With a glance in Lillian's direction, he saw that she was deep in conversation with Gran and Resnick. Deeming it safe, he shared his thoughts with Daryna.

Her expression smoothed after a moment, a soft smile

gracing her lips. "I do not think we need to fear Divine judgment or wrath. Most of what has unfolded in this lifetime is a direct result of the Battle Goddess's meddling. If any deserve punishment, it is her."

Daryna glanced away from him, looking off into the horizon. When she spoke again, it was in a voice that held a bitter tinge to it. "And we know the Divine Ones have never been able to call to heel their wildest child. What we have done is minor in comparison."

Her words might ring with truth, but that didn't mean he felt any better.

However, he didn't have time to dwell on it now. The teams that would be hunting him and his protégés were already in position. Gregory dropped to all fours and loped over to where the other gargoyles waited. It was going to be another long day. He could feel it in his bones.

CHAPTER TWENTY

*L*illian was just moving in for the 'kill,' her sights set on one of the new soldiers recently assigned to the training units when a magical disturbance raced across all her senses.

Shadowlight, Anna, and Gregory all froze in place and looked to the east. They'd felt it, too. Whatever 'it' was. Gregory lunged up to stand on two legs while he dropped his cloaking magic. Effectively appearing out of thin air in front of the soldiers.

He held up a hand and addressed the soldier closest to him.

"Inform Major Resnick and the other human leaders that someone, or even several individuals, have just arrived in the Mortal Realm. And they are not allies." Gregory turned toward Lillian. "Those newcomers can only be here at the Battle Goddess's behest. I imagine they're here to find out what happened to their commander as well as

River and Darkness. When they learn of Gryton's defeat and Darkness's death, they'll try to capture River."

"But why come now? Surely the Battle Goddess isn't yet ready for a full-scale war."

"This is most likely reconnaissance on our enemies' part. But do not fear. The spell Daryna and I wove around the hamadryad will have captured and transported them to the holding spell well outside of town. I'll deal with these interlopers."

"We'll rally the humans and go together," Lillian said with growing unease.

Gregory shook his head. "No, I want you to stay well away from the danger. Play fighting with the humans is one thing; battling a real enemy is something else altogether. I won't allow you to risk your life or that of our unborn child."

Lillian's hand crept down to the curve of her stomach. The concept of a child was so new, she often forgot she was pregnant. She barely showed and she didn't feel that different. But the tiny life was strong within her. While she wanted to be stubborn, she wouldn't risk her child either. "Very well. I'll stay behind."

"Daryna will transport you, Shadowlight, and Anna back to the hamadryad. The tree has some of the most powerful shielding. The Mother's Sorceress will stay behind to protect you in the off chance one of the enemies manages to get past me."

"What about you? You don't know how many you will be facing."

"I'll take a small army of human soldiers to face the

newcomers. Once the enemy has been neutralized, I will call you to me."

Lillian stepped up to Gregory and gave him a hug. Nuzzling him, she inhaled his scent, drawing it deep into her lungs. Letting him go was hard, but she did.

"You be careful and make sure you come back to us in one piece." Lillian stepped back and allowed Daryna to take her place.

The other woman stood on tiptoes until Gregory bowed his muzzle a few inches. Daryna pressed a lingering kiss to the side of Gregory's cheek. For once, the usual jealousy didn't manifest; Lillian was too worried about her mate's well-being.

Daryna smiled up at Gregory. "As my firstborn body has already said, be safe and return to us. I will keep all the young ones safe while you deal with the enemy."

Gregory huffed softly and then nodded. With one more glance at Lillian, he turned and dropped to all fours. With a powerful leap, he broke into a ground-devouring run. Within seconds he was out of sight, but Lillian could still follow his progress in her mind.

"Come, we need to go to the hamadryad," Daryna urged. "We'll guard her just in case any of the enemies get past Gregory. Once they realize they don't have the element of surprise and are outnumbered, they will seek to escape back to the Magic Realm to inform the Battle Goddess what is really going on here."

Lillian found herself actually nodding in agreement to something the Mother's Sorceress said. Together with Shadowlight and Anna, Lillian hung back while Daryna summoned a strange portal in the air. The spell shifted and swirled with bright flashes of magic for about ten seconds and then it calmed, forming a door in the air. On the other side was the south entrance to her maze.

Daryna called to them and walked on through. Lillian, Anna, and Shadowlight each glanced at the other and then with the equivalent of a group shrug, they crossed into the portal one at a time and out the other side, back to civilization.

She'd just emerged from the portal when armored vehicles came rolling up to the entrance. Major Resnick jumped out of one before it had come to a full stop. Daryna explained what was happening while ushering them all into the maze.

A few minutes later, Lillian found herself again in the shadow of her hamadryad tree. Daryna stood just inside the stone ring. Magic shimmered in the air around her as she added another layer of powerful shields to what was already anchored to the stone ring.

Outside the ring of standing stones, more soldiers waited, alert and ready to target anything or anyone they didn't know.

Anna stood apart from the other soldiers but was dressed in combat gear, with one of the modified military rifles resting in her hands. The ward-spell glowed an eerie green even in the bright light of day.

Shadowlight paced a circle around Anna, his tail flicking in agitation or perhaps eagerness. Lethal little shards of obsidian shadow magic danced and spun around him, awaiting his command to bite deep into an enemy.

Lillian hated to break it to her little brother that if all went well, none of them would be catching so much as the scent of the enemy.

In theory. Not that anything in Lillian's life ever went according to plan.

Her eyes slid back toward Daryna where she was adding a second spell and then to Anna who was armed for Armageddon and checking her weapons for the third time. Shadowlight paced into her line of sight again. Lillian couldn't help but notice that very little of the boisterous child was in evidence; a vigilant gargoyle had replaced him.

Lillian reflexively checked her own harnesses, scabbards and twin swords, feeling a little less sure.

Even if Gregory defeated the newcomers, there was a good chance that Commander Gryton would feel the arrival of warriors from his realm. She feared that might be enough to draw him back out of hiding.

Lillian's gaze returned to Shadowlight again. She wished there was a place they could stash the young gargoyle where he'd be safe, but nowhere was truly safe from Gryton, as he'd proven in the past. He'd once ventured into Lillian's own home.

In the future, they'd have to think of some kind of super-powered safe room where they could secure Shadowlight until the danger was past. But for now, Lillian supposed the best way to keep him safe was to keep him near one of the Avatars.

Still, she wished there was somewhere safer for him far from a potential battlefield.

"Anna, once this is over, remind me to talk to Gregory about building a safe room for Shadowlight."

The soldier side-eyed Lillian and then turned her attention to Shadowlight with a snort. "And who is going to sit on him to make sure he stays put?"

It wasn't lost on Lillian that making a safe room and getting Shadowlight to stay there would be two separate problems.

Anna's expression still held a hint of humor, but otherwise, the soldier was all business. A slight flare in the magic current drew Lillian's attention back to the Sorceress.

Daryna was just lowering her arms to her sides when their gazes met. She nodded for Lillian to come closer.

Lillian flicked a wing in annoyance at being summoned but came forward as she was bid.

"Do you want to watch Gregory while he battles the enemy?" Daryna asked as she held out her right hand.

While Lillian could sense his thoughts and track his location to some extent, she wasn't always able to see through his eyes now that she was no longer the Mother's Sorceress. The greater the distance, the fainter her link to him.

Of course I want to know what Gregory is doing! As her manipulative, meddling doppelgänger was well aware.

Outwardly, Lillian merely nodded her head and reached out for the other woman's hand.

When their fingers touched, Lillian's vision darkened unnaturally for a moment before a new location blurred into being.

"Where am—?" Lillian started to ask but felt Gregory's

mind. She was there with him mentally, seeing what he was seeing. He acknowledged her arrival with a spike of warm joy.

Somewhat uncertainly, Lillian formed words in her mind. *"Am I a distraction? I don't want my presence to endanger you."*

Gregory's warm joy sharpened into thoughts and words that soon filled her mind.

"You are always a welcome distraction, my beloved. However, to make things easier, stay silent once I engage the enemy," he paused and lifted his muzzle high while he sprinted between two military vehicles.

She sensed he was trying to learn something of the enemies by catching some news upon the breeze, but the stink of fumes from the vehicles disguised anything the wind might have carried.

Gregory put on a burst of speed and bolted ahead of the vehicles on either side.

His mind turned toward hers again. *"I can smell nothing of the enemy, but I can feel them working to free themselves from my trap. They've already managed to damage it, and that tells me the Lady of Battles has not sent just any grunts for this task. These are powerful magic wielders. While perhaps not as powerful as Gryton, still lethal. But I won't allow them past me."*

Lillian found herself nodding even though Gregory wouldn't be able to see it. *"I know. You will be victorious over these new enemies, and I will be here to mend your wounds—but please don't get hurt too badly. You know I hate seeing you in pain."*

Gregory laughed. *"I will keep that in mind. And while I do love how you look after my battle-weary body, I don't actually like pain, so will do my best to minimize the number of scars."*

"Thank you," Lillian whispered. She allowed her consciousness to drift. Gregory was still in her mind, but no longer forefront. She blinked, and her hamadryad's glade came back into view.

Anna and Shadowlight were still where they'd been all along, so too were the other soldiers. Only Daryna had moved to stand off to one side, her right hand now caressing one of the standing stones.

"Thank you," Lillian said as she glanced at Daryna.

"Thanks are never needed. I exist to help you and Gregory overthrow the Battle Goddess."

When had overthrowing the Battle Goddess become part of the plan?

Last she'd heard, the plan was to stop the Battle Goddess's army and prevent her from breeding a legion of new gargoyle hybrids. There had been no mention of actually attempting to destroy the Battle Goddess. Which come to think of it, Lillian would be totally cool with.

But she'd thought the Divine Ones had wanted the Twins to learn some kind of moral lesson. Unless Lillian had misunderstood something, the Mother Goddess and the All-Father weren't willing to kill their child. So why was the Mother's Sorceress now talking about destroying the Lady of Battles?

After the battle, Lillian would get Gregory alone and mention what Daryna had said. Or perhaps she would speak with the banshee first and see if the Fae had learned anything new.

CHAPTER TWENTY-ONE

As they neared the location of the trap, Gregory darted off the road and into the forest. He led close to fifty Fae who answered the call. They would circle wide and flank the enemy while the human soldiers would come from the South and East.

Dire wolves ran with elks and stags. There was even a moose carrying Greenborrow into battle with him. Gran rode the unicorn bareback while holding her staff in one hand. Gregory admired the elder's skill and was glad to have her ride into battle beside him.

On Gregory's left, the pooka ran on silent hooves, a predatory shadow just waiting to grind the bones of his enemies beneath his hooves.

The pooka's single-mindedness brought a smile to Gregory's lips. The pony was not the only one looking forward to the coming battle.

Gregory was more than ready to face a real opponent

after all the play hunting that he'd been doing as part of the cubs' training.

And perhaps it was a touch juvenile, but Lillian was with him in his mind, watching what he did, and he wanted to impress her. Or at least live up to his own reputation, which, of late, was somewhat tarnished since coming to this realm.

This felt a little like leading his gargoyles into battle. Something he'd missed since coming to the Mortal Realm.

"We are nearly there." He'd been about to explain strategy but halted as his attention was diverted. There was something wrong with one of the anchor-stones he'd created to lock the spell to this realm.

Even over the distance, he could feel the pressure building in the anchor. A heartbeat later, stress fractures formed along the heated stone.

A second and third anchor-stone now flared warnings at him.

Damn. The trap wasn't going to hold long enough for the Fae and military of this realm to get there in time.

There were over a dozen soldiers left to guard the anchor-stones and half again that number of Fae.

He glanced at Gran. "My trap is weakening and whatever is within has almost escaped. To do that so quickly, the newcomers must be fiercely powerful. The Fae and military stationed there won't have a chance and will be wiped out if I don't get there in the next few moments."

Gregory called power from the Spirit Realm as he put on a burst of speed.

"Wait! What are you doing? Lillian will kill you if you mess yourself up again."

"Stay the course. I'm going to help those already on location. Meet me there when you can."

Behind him Gran cursed, but he continued to surge ahead, calling more power as he ran. He leaped into the air and spread his wings. One powerful beat and then a second and he was airborne. However, he had no intention of flying the distance.

Ahead, the magic he'd summoned from the Spirit Realm shimmered and churned. Moments before he would have collided with it, the spell snapped into being, opening a rift. On the other side was the dome shaped trap he'd created.

Gunfire reached his sensitive ears, and he knew his trap had been breached by one or more of the invaders if the humans were engaging.

Two more powerful wing beats propelled him through the rift.

Below, it was as he expected. A pair of the invaders had managed to fight their way through the burning shield of energy. Ten more armor-clad warriors were still confined within the trap but were working their way through the multilayered shield as he watched.

He swooped down on one of the warriors as he started toward the nearest anchor-stone.

The stones were outside Gregory's trap, so he hadn't added much in the way of protection, just enough to keep curious Fae and military scientists at bay.

Gunfire rang out again, which reminded Gregory not to

summon his shadow magic to hide his approach. He'd felt the sting of the humans' bullets enough to respect the tiny shards of metal. Getting winged by 'friendly fire' as Major Resnick called it, wasn't something he needed.

He was going to get roughed up enough as it was.

The armor-clad figure continued toward his target, unaware Gregory was diving for him.

At the last minute, Gregory unfurled his wings and changed the angle of his descent to intercept the enemy.

They collided with a leaden thump, Gregory's weight and momentum driving the other off his feet and together they continued backward a good twenty meters until the solid energy of the dome stopped them.

Power snapped and hissed, at which point Gregory realized the warrior's armor was an iron mix of some kind.

Ah. That's why they'd been able to force their way through his shield. A second realization occurred to him as he grappled with the invader. This creature—whatever he fought—wasn't of Fae lineage. None of the Fae could wear armor such as this.

His impact had dented the other's armor, and Gregory took advantage of the warped breastplate to pry up a corner near the arm. With a bit of work, Gregory managed to sink a few claws into exposed tissue.

Blood gushed, and the other male screamed.

Good, they could feel pain and they could bleed, which also meant they could die.

They grappled with each other as the battle continued around them. He fought his opponent with lethal blows intended to end the fight quickly. There were eleven more opponents besides the one he fought. But the humans were keeping this one's partners busy at least.

Gregory worked the hole in his opponent's armor bigger. Then summoning Spirit Magic, he channeled it into the opening. The scent of blood and burnt flesh clogged his nose, but above all that he could smell the taint of a demon. This one was not Riven, but something else.

Apparently, the Battle Goddess had not learned her lesson from the Riven. Gregory wondered how long these hybrid demons would serve her before they, too, betrayed her like the Riven had.

Well, she wouldn't have to worry about this fellow's betrayal. Spirit Magic continued to build within the armor. Trapped, it had nowhere to go since the armor was designed to prevent magic from entering, or, in this case, exiting.

Gregory delivered a powerful kick and knocked the other male away seconds before the warrior screamed in high pitched agony. A moment later, demon, host, and armor all vaporized in a flash of bright magic. Sparks flew in all directions as the iron-mix armor melted into a molten slag. It splashed against his own shields and the surrounding area like wind-driven rain.

Smoke rose up from the dry grass as a few tiny curls of flame appeared. Gregory waved at the small fires, extinguishing them before they could grow dangerous.

He was darting forward to tackle the other opponent on this side of the dome when the energy flickered and flared wildly before it winked out of existence.

Ten more enemies rushed forward from inside the shattered ring of anchor-stones.

Oh. Lillian was going to be pissed at him.

With a joyous roar, he charged toward them, his shadow magic darting before him. He collided with the fastest of the newcomers and tore his helmet from his head. A blast of Spirit magic took care of that fellow and Gregory was leaping forward again.

But the others had seen what he'd done to two of their number, so swiftly drew back out of his way. He summoned more shadow magic and set it hunting. Most of the small shards were unable to get past the protections worked into the enemies' armor, but it confused them and slowly herded them where Gregory wanted his next opponent.

Leaping forward, he bounded into a group of three enemies. While he blocked their blows with magic, he ripped at their armor and looked for other weaknesses he could exploit that would allow him to dispatch them swiftly.

As he drove his present opponents back, gouging and tearing into breastplates, helmets and shoulder guards, the rest converged upon him and joined the fight. Gregory broke off the attack before their combined axes and swords could cut him to pieces.

Several armed military vehicles rolled into the meadow. Massive guns mounted on the backs took aim at the enemy. A second later, more gunfire tore through the air. The noise was enough he was surprised the air itself didn't shatter like glass under the onslaught.

Unfortunately, the Battle Goddess's soldiers had

powerful personal shields that stopped the bullets. But the sheer force and number prevented the enemy from spreading out. Ah. They were combining their power. They weren't strong enough individually.

Gregory circled around behind, preventing the enemy from retreating.

That's when he saw Gran and the other Fae arriving. They swiftly joined the military already in place. Then the two forces, both magical and mortal, focused their efforts on one enemy at a time. Gregory felt mild pride at how well they fought together. Perhaps the training sessions were beneficial, after all.

CHAPTER TWENTY-TWO

*L*illian piggybacked on Daryna's link to Gregory, and together they shared in his vision of the battle. Neither woman said anything to distract him. The last thing he needed was to have his attention divided.

While she was glad to at least know what was going on, Lillian wished to be fighting by his side. She would have been if not for the tiny, fragile life within her womb. Not that she regretted her baby, not for a moment. She just wanted Gregory safe, too.

Lillian was drawing breath to demand Daryna go to his aid when military reinforcements and the other Fae arrived. The tension between her shoulder blades eased a touch, and she rolled them to try to further loosen up the stiff muscles. Still, her wings twitched with nervousness.

Daryna tilted her head to the side suddenly, like she

was listening to something Lillian could not hear. She strained her senses, and then she felt it.

Another tremor of magic shivered through the air.

"Did you feel that?"

Daryna blinked open her eyes. "Yes. I did. It's not good news, I fear."

Lillian felt her talons flex. "Speak."

"It's more of the Battle Goddess's warriors."

Just what they didn't need. Then she knew why Daryna looked so torn. "Go to Gregory. He'll need your help."

"I can't leave you and our child unprotected."

Flashing a hint of fang in a wicked gargoyle grin, Lillian stared down at Daryna and tightened her hold on her swords' hilts. "While I may not be as lethal as either you or Gregory, I am not helpless. Besides, I also have Anna, Shadowlight, the banshee and a shit ton of military just waiting for a chance to get some of the Battle Goddess's soldiers in their crosshairs."

Her tail flicked slowly back and forth while she waited for Daryna to answer. Perhaps she needed another nudge. "How much more danger do you think I'll be in if Gregory and the others get more than they can handle? If even one or two of those enemies escaped, where do you think they're going to head next?"

"They'll come for the hamadryad. My spells will prevent them from traveling back to the Magic Realm, but if they are able to get close enough, they will be able to send a message requesting reinforcements. If the Battle Goddess thinks she has a chance to get a foothold in the Mortal Realm, she might act now even if she isn't finished building her army. We must stop them before they can get close."

"Go then. Help Gregory neutralize the enemy before they can endanger all the earth."

Daryna nodded. Looking unhappy, she moved away from Lillian until she was outside the ring of stones. Moments later she summoned another portal spell; its magic was like a cold draft from the Spirit Realm. For the span of ten heartbeats Lillian saw nothing, and then the strange magic doorway solidified and beyond the threshold was the place where a bloody battle was underway.

Daryna glanced back over her shoulder at Lillian. "Stay."

She would have made the retort that she wasn't a dog, but the Sorceress stepped through the portal and was already summoning a deadly spell. The strange doorway collapsed before Lillian had a chance to see what shape the combat spell took.

"Being left behind still sucks," Lillian hissed under her breath.

Anna's snort told Lillian the hybrid had heard her. The other woman sauntered over and glanced where the portal had been. "You think it was a good idea to send her to the others? From the updates Resnick is getting over the radio, the battle is going well. The training sessions have paid off."

"Daryna said that if even one of the enemy soldiers gets close to the hamadryad, they'll be able to use her to call for reinforcements."

"A tree that doubles as a long-range radio. Yep.

Normal," Anna said but glanced around the meadow distractedly.

Lillian noticed Anna's fingers flexed on her weapon. A show of nervousness? That wasn't normal.

"Do you sense something?" *If so, why the hell didn't you say something before I sent Daryna away?*

"No, but it's never a good idea to send all your big guns into battle and leave your forward operating base unprotected," Anna countered and then sighed. "It's nothing. Just all this magic putting me on edge. I'm really starting to hate magic."

Lillian flashed a fang at Anna. "You sound a lot like I did when I first learned about all this, but I've gained friends that I wouldn't have found otherwise. You'll see the benefits one day, too.

"Sorry. Don't believe in silver linings." Anna's gaze flicked over to where Shadowlight was walking a perimeter around the tree. He was looking all fierce and daunting again. "Well, maybe the kid. He might be worth every poke and prod I've received from the scientists. Maybe."

"I heard that!" Shadowlight huffed and galloped over to them. "Of course I'm worth it. You've always wanted a little brother."

She smiled affectionately at the gargoyle. "Yeah, kid. I've got one now, and you're correct. I wouldn't change anything."

Wiggling happily, Shadowlight bounded around Anna. He'd been about to say something else but was cut short by a soft whistling sound that ended in something small smacking into flesh.

Shadowlight whirled around in surprise, but the sound occurred twice more. The young gargoyle twisted and pulled three small darts from his flank. They rested tiny and guiltless in his palm.

What the hell?

A commotion among the soldiers had Lillian glancing away from her brother for a moment, in time to see two soldiers dropped to the ground.

The high-pitched sound came again, and more soldiers fell before the tiny darts. Lillian still didn't fully understand what was happening when Goswin stepped from out of the maze's west entrance. She fired more darts from a small blowpipe.

Every dart that found a target dropped a soldier to the ground.

Lillian decided she didn't *need* to know what was going on. All she needed to know was that a sprite was a swift and deceptively deadly little Fae.

And worse, she wasn't alone. Whitethorn, leader of The Hunt, walked in beside her and took aim with a much larger and more deadly bow and arrow.

Grabbing Anna, Lillian dragged her behind the hamadryad. From within the screen of the thick branches, Lillian saw something far more serious than just the two Fae.

Commander Gryton paced along behind them, tossing his fiery magic at anything that still moved.

Anna called Shadowlight to them, and he obeyed, but Lillian noticed he was none too steady on his feet. He tripped as much as stopped next to Anna. The human stepped over him and put herself between him and the threat.

"We are so screwed," Lillian muttered to herself. Anna didn't disagree with her and was already on the radio calling for reinforcements.

"We need to buy some time until more help gets here." Anna took aim with her rifle and the sharp report of weapons fire echoed through the glade.

Lillian winced at the sharp noise but focused her attention on the battle. Anna ignored Whitethorn and Goswin and fired rapid bursts at Commander Gryton. She knew who the true threat was.

Four other soldiers who had managed to dodge darts, arrows, and Gryton's fireballs, joined in the fight. Together the five soldiers managed to slow Gryton. Halting him was like stopping a flow of lava. He continued to walk forward, pushing a wall of fire in front of him.

The fiery wall seemed to turn most of the bullets into molten slag, which splattered against his armor with dull, wet sounds.

But Anna and the other soldiers didn't give up, holding their positions and continuing to fire. Now and again, a sharp ting sounded and a few sparks flew as bullets made it past Gryton's defensive magic to strike his armor.

Whitethorn stepped out from around the wall of fire as he drew his bowstring and took aim at one of the soldiers.

Lillian called her shadow magic and shaped it into tiny, biting, knife-like shards. The bits of darkness raced across the distance and savaged Whitethorn. The sidhe huntsman dove for cover behind a stone picnic table, but Lillian's magic followed.

So too did Shadowlight. The young gargoyle lunged from behind the cover of the hamadryad and raced across the distance. He jumped the picnic table and closed his teeth upon Whitethorn, shaking the other Fae in his jaws. While Shadowlight was fighting Whitethorn, Goswin got in another dart.

Lillian growled and lunged after the sprite, her shadow magic racing before her. The sprite was faster and darted behind one of the stone rings.

A moment later she popped up and fired two more darts at the soldiers. One struck the soldier nearest Anna. He staggered and then dropped to his knees. A second soldier joined his fellow.

Before any of the allies could regroup, a wave of force raced out from where Gryton stood. This wasn't the fire magic that Lillian had expected, but Anna and the other remaining soldiers were still knocked off their feet.

Bad. Very bad, Lillian thought as she summoned more shadow magic and directed it to attack Gryton.

Her magic was marginally more effective than the bullets. Like tiny bits of shrapnel, they burrowed their way into the seams of his armor. He couldn't stop them all.

Gryton snarled at her but turned his attention toward Shadowlight, ignoring Lillian.

What the hell?

Then she understood.

Oh, hell no.

Anna had regained her feet, but the other soldiers were

unmoving. Shaking her head like her ears were ringing or she was disoriented, Anna shook off whatever the attack had done to her as she raised her rifle once more.

This time, her target was Goswin, where she stood over Shadowlight. Blood blossomed at the sprite's shoulder and then her thigh. She screamed as she fell. She tried to regain her feet but couldn't.

Two down, Lillian thought, just one really badass enemy to go.

With a growl, Anna redirected her fire upon Gryton. Lillian joined her. Their combined assault slowed but didn't stop him.

Not that it should have, Lillian knew. Before, Gryton had very nearly been a match for Gregory.

Strangely, he didn't seem to be pressing his advantage. The Battle Goddess's most deadly weapon should have made short work of Anna and herself. Why hadn't he dealt them a crippling blow? So far, everything he'd tossed at them was more defensive magic than bring-your-enemies-to-their-knees lethal.

Was he weakened by something the hamadryad had done to him?

Or was this something else?

Then Lillian realized he must want to capture more than just Shadowlight.

There was an abrupt end to the gunfire, and the resulting absence of sound announced their defeat. Lillian's ears twitched at the lack of painful noise, but she didn't hesitate and continued her attack upon Gryton. Unfortunately, Anna was out of bullets, and they were out of options.

And then Lillian felt yet another disturbance in the magic around her like she had twice before in the last hour.

A churning vortex appeared in the air between Anna and Gryton. For a moment, Lillian felt hope rekindle. If Gregory was here...

But it wasn't Gregory.

CHAPTER TWENTY-THREE

hree more armor-clad warriors stepped into the glade and shouted something at Gryton. They didn't sound overly friendly, and neither did Gryton's reply. Lillian had the distinct impression that Commander Gryton was surprised by these newcomers' sudden appearance. He wasn't the only one.

Lillian moved closer to Anna, thinking to grab her and fly to safety. But one glance at Shadowlight told Lillian that that plan wasn't going to work either.

Shadowlight was on his feet again, but he was weaving and stumbling badly and he collapsed after a couple more steps. He fought against whatever drug, poison, or magic spell the darts had delivered into his system and struggled back to his feet. Lillian's heart broke. The youngling was trying to reach them. But he was in no condition to fly or run.

Lillian dropped to all fours and snarled at Gryton. She had to get to Shadowlight. When she tried to circle around the armor-clad enemy, he snapped out his wrists and a wave of power raced toward her.

She dove to the ground and dug in her claws as the wave rolled over her. It continued past to flow harmlessly away. While Lillian and Gryton danced around each other uselessly, the three newcomers marched straight for Shadowlight. Two of them grabbed him under his arms and started dragging him toward the portal.

Shadowlight twisted and fought, but in his drugged state he was no match for them and was quickly clubbed into submission.

Anna snarled and tossed away her empty rifle and pulled out a long knife instead. Her expression was fierce and unreasoning as she charged across the distance. At the last moment, she hunched low and tackled one of the newcomers hard enough to make a linebacker proud.

The warrior crashed to the ground, and Anna followed, her knife finding the slit in the enemy's visor. Blood sprayed. The newcomer screamed. Anna's knife flashed again and again until the body under her stopped twitching.

Apparently, not all the Battle Goddess's warriors were as hard to kill as Gryton.

Lillian darted across the distance, angling toward the two who still dragged Shadowlight between them. Anna joined her, sprinting toward the enemy from the right. They had almost reached their targets when the ground heaved under Lillian's feet, and a secondary force slammed into her back.

Earth and sky changed places over and over. She continued to roll until her maze's evergreen walls caught her. The scent of cedar surrounded her. Lillian blinked and spit out a mouthful of dirt, grass, and bits of cedar. What had hit her? A wrecking ball?

She shook her head. After a moment, she blinked her vision clear. Gryton was bent over Anna, and then he heaved her up into his arms and over his shoulder. The other two dragging Shadowlight had almost reached the portal.

Gryton glanced at her, clearly wanting to snatch Lillian as well, but decided against it as he turned and walked toward the portal.

He didn't make it. A second portal appeared between him and his destination.

A raging ball of gargoyle fury erupted out of the portal and lunged right at Commander Gryton. At first, Lillian thought Shadowlight had escaped his captors, but then she recognized her beloved Gregory.

Relief washed through her. She tried to get to her feet and go to him, but her body didn't want to cooperate. Helpless, she could only watch through her narrowing field of vision as the two lethal predators squared off.

By the rising scent of deadly magic filling her glade, Lillian could only conclude that Gryton had no interest in capturing Gregory. And Gregory's snarls told Lillian that her beloved had no interest in leaving this enemy alive.

Another portal flared brightly and Daryna walked out

of it into the battle-scarred glade. Magic burned all along her body, and she stood and took aim at the two dragging Shadowlight back to the Magic Realm.

The first wave slammed into a shield and scattered in twenty different directions. Daryna didn't stop and continued forward undaunted, tossing another wave of magic at the enemy. The two enemy soldiers scrambled the rest of the way to the portal and were through it before Lillian could cry out.

Daryna screamed in rage, but the other portal was already closing in upon itself, its magic shimmering less brightly as the portal diminished in size. She darted forward but was already too late.

With a hiss of anger, she turned to where Gryton and Gregory still fought. She raised her arms, palms toward the two combatants.

Gryton's survival instincts must have been truly impressive for he broke away from Gregory and lunged behind one of the standing stones that circled the hamadryad. A moment after he vanished behind the stone, Lillian again felt a disturbance in the magic around her. There was also the thick, fiery essence she'd come to associate with a spike of Gryton's power.

But it was already fading. And that's when she realized Gryton had vanished from her senses.

Gregory stomped around behind the standing stone, but his thunderous expression told Lillian what she already knew. Gryton was gone. Escaped.

Tin Man had more lives than a freaking cat.

One day she was going to do her best to chew through

all nine of them. But not today. Today they had to go after Shadowlight. Lillian just had to stand up first. If her body would cooperate. Unfortunately, she was also losing the war against the darkness creeping up the edges of her vision. Her sight narrowed down further, and the glade faded.

CHAPTER TWENTY-FOUR

Anna came awake with a jerk as a bright light shone in her eyes. A field medic was kneeling next to her. She shoved him away, and her entire body screamed in pain as she rolled to her feet, but something, some need, drove her to alertness.

"Easy," the medic said. She ignored him.

There had been a battle.

Whitethorn and Goswin had turned on them.

Gryton.

Fucking Tin Man had attacked them again.

Shadowlight. She scanned the area, looking first to the hamadryad and then to where Daryna and Gregory stood over Lillian.

Anna glanced around to where the other medics were attending to more survivors.

Panic rising within her, she scanned the entire area

again, but still no Shadowlight. And a gargoyle was a bit hard to miss.

"Where is he?"

The medic grabbed her arm. "You took a beating. You probably have a concussion. Possibly internal bleeding."

"Get your hands off me, or you will be the one with internal bleeding."

Anna recognized one of the scientists approaching. She snarled, showing fangs. "Tell me what happened to Shadowlight?"

"We don't know," Doctor Fleming said.

Instinctively, Anna reached out for that blood-link she shared with Shadowlight. Normally there would be a tingle, or stronger tug, which would lead her to him.

But this time there was nothing. Just a void.

Oh, God. No.

Please, no. Not the kid.

He couldn't be dead.

Major Resnick entered the clearing leading another squad of soldiers. But Anna stormed past him. He was just arriving and wouldn't have the answers she needed. Instead, she headed directly toward Gregory and Daryna where they knelt next to Lillian.

Anna skidded to a halt beside them, her throat threatening to seal itself as grief welled up within her.

"Where is Shadowlight," she asked for the third time.

Three sets of eyes glanced up at her. Lillian was crying.

Oh, God. "Is he dead?"

White rage mixed with grief in her mind. If that bright, loveable goof had been snuffed out of the universe, she would…kill everything. Exterminate every last one of the Battle Bitch's godless henchmen. She'd start with Commander Gryton. She'd find a way.

Gregory didn't answer with words, but he shook his head.

Anna felt like the earth had just shifted under her feet. He wasn't dead? Oh, thank God.

If Shadowlight had been hurt, she'd see that he had all the care he needed to heal. She'd raid the town's library to find enough books to occupy him every damned hour of the day if he wanted her to read to him.

"He's hurt, isn't he? Where did they take him? Back to base?" He must have been bad off to leave her behind, Anna thought as another cold tendril of fear wormed its way into her heart.

Coming to her feet, Lillian stood on shaking legs, but still towered above Anna in gargoyle form. Gregory stayed on all fours, offering his back for his mate to lean upon.

Lillian ignored Gregory and reached out for Anna, dragging her into a hug. Surprised to find herself in a fierce and unexpected hug, Anna just patted the gargoyle's back awkwardly.

"They took Shadowlight. They took my little brother, and I couldn't stop them." Lillian drew in a ragged breath and continued, "Gregory and Daryna won't go after him. They won't let me go after him, either."

The other woman broke into great body-shaking sobs.

Gregory stood and wrapped her in his arms. Even Daryna came forward to place a comforting arm around her shoulders.

"We can't just leave him to become the Battle Goddess's slave," Lillian whispered between sobs.

"Of course we're not leaving Shadowlight in enemy hands. We'll launch a counter assault and get him back," Anna swung her attention back toward Resnick. She waved him over. "Resnick is here. He'll inform the others that Shadowlight has been taken. We'll get him back."

Anna wasn't sure if her words were meant to comfort herself or Lillian.

"Gregory and Daryna won't allow anyone else to go after him, either." The accusation was clear in her voice.

The demigods wouldn't allow anyone to go?

Well, fuck that.

"We won't leave Shadowlight to the Battle Goddess's mercy. We can't. We can't risk him sharing everything we've done here. Even if they do not want to risk themselves or others, we still must send a team to rescue Shadowlight."

Daryna stepped away from Lillian to study Anna instead. "It's not as easy as you make it sound. Anyone who attempts to invade the Battle Goddess's territory would be found out and incarcerated. When we move on her, we must be ready to strike a blow she won't recover from."

"What are you saying?" Although, Anna thought she knew what the Sorceress was telling her.

Falling silent, Daryna paced a half circle around Anna. "We are simply not ready to go after Shadowlight. Your fellow humans are not ready for a full-scale war to land in their backyard, either."

"So, you will do nothing?" Anna heard her own voice climb an octave. She couldn't lose her shit over this. Shadowlight needed her calm, composed, and focused on his rescue.

"We will not be doing nothing," Daryna said as she continued to pat Lillian's back. "We will be readying for battle. And I promise you, when we are ready to strike a devastating blow, we will find Shadowlight and free him from the Battle Goddess's traps."

But Shadowlight might not have the time. Anna couldn't imagine the Battle Goddess sitting back and waiting for Shadowlight to reveal what he knew. He would be tortured for information.

"Daryna is correct," Gregory said. "We can't risk open war with the Battle Goddess yet. She might very well win. And we don't dare appear in the Battle Goddess's domain until after we have an army ready and eager to destroy hers. We must approach Shadowlight's rescue with caution."

"But I can't sit back and allow any number of horrors to be performed upon the kid."

Gregory's voice softened. "We will go after Shadowlight. But as much as my every instinct is screaming to go after him now, we need a plan, as well as an idea of what traps we may be up against. If we have any hope of rescuing Shadowlight, we will need to know what to expect and get in and out quickly without being discovered."

Anna felt a tiny bit of hope. It wasn't that Gregory was abandoning Shadowlight, he just needed a sound plan.

Worry and guilt still churned within her, but she managed to calm some of the rage. Although the need to beat the shit out of something was still strong.

She would get Shadowlight back.

Gregory nudged Lillian gently, trying to coax her into climbing onto his back. When she refused, Gregory continued his earlier line of thought. "I might not know exactly what the Battle Goddess has been up to, but I know someone who does. Tomorrow I will hunt down Gryton, drag him back here, and carve out every piece of information we need."

Anna arched her brow. How was he going to capture Tin Man? That bastard was slipperier than shit and disappeared faster than fog in the summer. So far, he'd proven impossible to catch.

"This is the second time we've managed to get a chunk of him." Gregory held up a piece of battered and blood-stained armor. "With this, I have enough of his blood and magic to create a spell to track him. He will not be able to hide from me this time. His armor is a physical manifestation of his power. It's a part of him."

"I'll help," Anna said as that intense need to protect Shadowlight reared up within her again.

"No. Not this time. I'll not risk losing another cub to Gryton's tricks."

"I'm not a cub."

"You are not even a quarter-century old." Gregory huffed. "A cub."

Her teeth creaked as she ground them together. Who wasn't a child compared to this immortal demigod's age? Anna tried another tactic. "I'm older than Lillian—"

He cut her off. "Lillian isn't going either. Daryna will stay behind to guard you both while I hunt down Gryton." There was a long stretch of silence as he eyed his sorceress.

"Daryna will remain to guard you this time. No matter what."

Anna was somewhat surprised to hear the harsh tone directed at Daryna.

Huh? So, the male half of the demigod pairing could and would get pissed off at his female half.

If Anna wasn't so worried about Shadowlight, she might have investigated that more.

"How long do you need to track down Gryton?"

"A few hours. But I must look over Lillian to make sure she and our child are both well. And the humans will want to be brought up to date." Gregory glanced at the darkening sky. "I'll start the hunt at dawn after I've had a chance to make sure Lillian is fully healed."

"I'm fine," the other woman piped up, "we can start the hunt now."

"No," Gregory said in a deep rumble as he wrapped Lillian in the protective shelter of his wings. "I felt your pain and desperation during the battle with Gryton. You need healing."

"I'll be fine. I'm a gargoyle. My body is already healing."

Daryna laid a hand over Lillian's abdomen. "He's worried about our child."

That got Lillian's attention. Her tail stopped flicking and her wings wrapped around herself as if that would help protect her unborn child.

Anna wasn't the maternal type. Didn't want kids. And yet she still felt a strong, soul-deep sympathy for the poor woman.

Out loud, Anna added, "Let Gregory take care of you.

Then he won't be distracted when he goes to hunt down Gryton. I'll get Resnick up to speed with the situation."

Because, by God, if Anna wasn't given a job, she was going to lose her shit. She couldn't help it. The need to rescue the kid was almost overwhelming.

"Thank you," Lillian said.

Gregory and Daryna supported Lillian between them as they walked from the maze.

Anna was left with a very unhappy looking Resnick. He stopped before her, frowned down at her, and then took in the scene. "Don't get me wrong. I'm happy to see you alive. But what the hell happened? I'm getting conflicting reports. Start talking."

Anna stood at attention. "Yes, sir."

At least telling him everything she knew gave her a purpose.

CHAPTER TWENTY-FIVE

*L*illian allowed Daryna and Gregory to help her back to the cottage. Once there, Gregory simply pulled her into his arms and carried her up to their rooms. No small feat since she was still in her gargoyle form and was as tall as him, if not quite as heavily muscled.

Daryna kept pace with them and Lillian's battered body drank in the healing power of the Mother's Sorceress. At the moment, she couldn't summon a speck of anger or distrust for Daryna. She was just happy to have help, since it might be the difference between life and death for her unborn child.

Once they entered the master bedroom, Gregory carried her to the bed and sat down with her. He kept her in his lap, his wings and arms circling her protectively.

"Is our child all right?" Lillian directed the question at both Daryna and Gregory, not caring who answered.

Daryna dropped down in front of Lillian and gripped her wrists. Taking a pulse? Weaving more magic?

"Our little one is strong," she said as she glanced between Lillian and Gregory. "All is well. Although, sleep will certainly be beneficial." Again, Daryna paused. "Are you sure you don't wish to know our child's gender?"

"You can tell already?"

"Yes. Gargoyle offspring develop much faster than humans."

"I..." Lillian began but paused and let her hands drop to her stomach. She wanted this baby to be a surprise. But more importantly, she didn't want to associate this new life with darkness or unhappiness. Now, with Shadowlight captured, it was far from a joyous time.

But what did Gregory want?"

Lillian turned just enough so she could look up at him. "Do you wish to know?"

His muzzle dipped down to nuzzle her hair and lower still to caress her cheek. "No. I believe there should still be some mysteries in the universe."

Lillian pressed a kiss to his cheek. "Good. A surprise it shall be."

She looked back to find Daryna's gaze turned inward, vague and far away.

"Are you well?" She asked the other woman just to see what kind of answer she'd get. "Drawing on power is damaging to you, isn't it?"

"I am well, but now that you are healed, you should get some rest. Gregory will stay with you while I go and meet with Vivian, Greenborrow, and the other Fae Council members. We need to find out and reverse whatever Gryton did to Whitethorn and Goswin.

Lillian nodded. The sooner the two Fae were freed from whatever spell had enslaved their minds, the better. What other powers did Gryton possess that they had yet to discover? She hadn't known Gryton had the ability to control another's mind.

"Very well," Daryna said. "I shall go. But when I return, I had better find you both fast asleep."

"Yes, my Sorceress," Gregory said in a respectful tone, but there was a mischievous glint in his eyes.

Daryna stood, gave Lillian one more probe with her magic, and then made her way toward the door.

After she was gone, Lillian reached out and wrapped Gregory's arms even more firmly around her body.

"I want a shower, but I also just want to be held," she admitted.

"I don't see why we can't do both," Gregory said as he nuzzled her hair again. "Although there is no way two gargoyles will fit in the shower. Do you feel up to shapeshifting back to your dryad form?"

Lillian sighed, not wanting to dredge up the strength required to shapeshift, but the thought of being clean swayed her into summoning her magic. After a few swift, mostly painless moments, her body morphed back into her smaller dryad form.

Gregory continued to nuzzle her hair and showered affection upon her, every so often his tongue would come out for a quick caress.

He soon stood up. With Lillian held easily in his arms,

he started to walk toward the bathroom. His long strides quickly covered half the distance. Lillian wrapped her arms around his neck and leaned up to brush her lips against his.

"Thank you for existing," Lillian whispered.

"Always. And we will get Shadowlight back."

CHAPTER TWENTY-SIX

The forest's night creatures were out, predators hunting on silent wings and stealthy paws. Her claws flexed and her fangs lengthened. Anna might have considered herself another predator if she had something to hunt.

But she was impotent without a target. She'd never felt so helpless.

She'd left HQ far behind and slipped silently into the surrounding woods with no one the wiser. For all Major Resnick knew, she had gone to get some much-needed rest. Which had been her original idea, but she couldn't sleep, couldn't even think about sleep while Shadowlight was still a prisoner.

She wanted to snarl at the night, at the many injustices of the world, but most especially at a cold-hearted demigoddess. Someone needed to eradicate the Battle Goddess.

That Gregory was willing to attempt a rescue was some relief. But not enough. She wanted to go with him and see Shadowlight freed. That might ease the tiniest portion of her guilt for failing the cub so terribly.

Unfortunately, Gregory's rescue mission hinged on catching Gryton and forcing him to cooperate. Catching Gryton might take days. Trusting him to help? Well, that would be never.

Which was why Anna found herself haunting the shadowy forest. She was too restless to sleep and perhaps too dangerous to her fellow humans to remain among them. Rational she was not.

A twig snapped to her left and the sounds of footsteps that hadn't been there a moment before reached her sensitive ears. When she focused on the direction of the sound, she could perceive a faint heartbeat and less than a minute later the familiar scent of Lillian or Daryna reached her nose. She wasn't sure which woman approached. Their scents were identical.

However, she'd learned to differentiate them by how they carried themselves. The Sorceress moved with superhuman grace; Lillian moved like your average human being.

When the woman finally walked into Anna's line of sight, she knew this was the powerful sorceress.

"Daryna." The one word came out almost a growl. Anna wasn't in the mood for company tonight.

"That's no way to greet the person who is about to help you rescue Shadowlight." The Sorceress halted before her, looking calm and confident as always. Anna scanned the area a second time, hunting for Gregory in the deepest shadows where the moonlight didn't penetrate the forest canopy. But there was no sign of the male demigod.

"I came alone," Daryna said as she held out a large rucksack that looked like it had been stolen from supplies.

Anna was more interested in what the other woman had said about Shadowlight and rescue than the rucksack's origin.

"How are you going to help me rescue Shadowlight? Did you and Gregory change your minds?"

"Come." Daryna gestured to a recently fallen tree some twenty meters away. "What I have planned will take some explanation."

Anna wanted to get to the meat of the matter. Circling around a subject always drove her nuts. And tonight, she was already too much on edge, but she stomped over to the tree in question and thumped her ass down upon it without uttering one damn word.

Daryna settled on the tree a good two feet away and brushed her hands along the tree's bark. "This one was far too young to fall. She was destroyed from within by a boring insect that caused rot to set in." Daryna paused and glanced sideways to meet Anna's gaze.

It took some fortitude to hold her gaze, but Anna did it.

To her surprise, Daryna looked away first and then said in a soft voice. "I can't sit by and watch the equivalent happen to Shadowlight."

There was guilt in her tone. Did the great demigod feel responsible for what happened to Shadowlight? Well, good, she should. They'd all failed the kid.

"You're going to go after him," Anna stated bluntly.

"Gregory would follow if I did. Also, this body is only temporary. It wouldn't withstand the force of magic that I'd be required to call upon to fight the Battle Goddess and rescue Shadowlight. And I can't tell you how bad it would be for this body to expire within the Goddess's domain where she could recapture my soul and force it to be reborn into another body of her choosing. Yet, I also fear Shadowlight might not be able to wait for Gregory."

"Then what do you have in mind?" Even as Anna said the words, an inkling came to her.

"Sometimes it is better to send one spy into enemy territory rather than an entire army."

Anna would go in a heartbeat, but she wasn't at all certain of her ability to get herself and Shadowlight free of the place. She would try. "Of course I'll go. But I will need supplies."

Daryna patted the rucksack she'd brought with her. "There is food, water, spare clothing, and blankets. You must get yourself weapons as I am unfamiliar with them. But I will create a map for you from my childhood memories. The basic structure and layout will be much the same but be aware whatever I draw will be twelve years out-of-date."

"It will do," Anna said, as new purpose filled her blood and enlivened her senses. "You could draw me a map in the dirt, and I still would agree to go for a chance to save Shadowlight."

"Oh. There is a catch, I'm afraid." Daryna reached into

her pack and rummaged around until she pulled out first one medallion and then a second and held them out.

With a questioning look, Anna took the offered objects and studied them both. She wasn't well-versed in magic, but she recognized power when she felt it. These were no mere ornaments.

"Locating Shadowlight within the Battle Goddess's temple will not be easy. Freeing him will be harder. And getting free again—I think you know the odds won't be in your favor."

"I don't care. I'll go. I'll do it and free Shadowlight or die trying."

"I can send you into the Magic Realm, and if your mission is successful, these medallions will allow you and Shadowlight to return here."

Anna turned the medallions this way and that. "How do these work?"

"They're really rather simple. You just smear a bit of blood on them to trigger the spell. They are actually keyed to Shadowlight's blood, but you now share some of that same blood, so the spell will recognize you as well."

Anna glanced down at them again. "That's it? Just bleed on them?"

"Yes. It will trigger the spell and transport you back to the Mortal Realm immediately."

"Got it." More weird shit, but she understood.

"I fear rescuing Shadowlight will not be easy. He will be under heavy guard." Daryna folded her fingers together and laid them in her lap. "Those guardians will be highly trained with as many well-developed senses as you now possess."

"Understood."

"There is one other thing. If it looks like you are about to be captured or you somehow lose the medallions before you get to Shadowlight, you still have another escape."

Great, more cryptic crap.

Daryna continued like she was unaware of Anna's impatience. "All gargoyles belong to the Lord of the Underworld. In a moment of desperate need, even you will be able to find your way to his temple."

"Not that I want to find myself there, but I'm a firm believer in having all scenarios thoroughly planned out. Is there a map to his realm?"

"The gateway is one found in your mind. Reach out to Lord Death and he will answer."

"Hmmm. Yep. Okay." Totally get in and get out without being discovered. Run like hell and then use the medallions.

Daryna's expression took on that distant look again. "There isn't much time. If we are going to do this, it needs to be now while Gregory is distracted attending to Lillian."

"I'll need some things first," Anna said, already building a supplies list in her mind.

"Take these."

Anna held out her hand and looked at what appeared to be flat discs of softened candle wax.

"Rub your fingers in this and then find a bit of exposed skin on your target and they will be unconscious before they hit the ground.

Anna glanced up at Daryna skeptically. "It won't affect me?"

"No. It will only affect those who don't share your genetic heritage."

"Hmmm. DNA targeted magic."

Daryna stood and walked forward until she was directly in front of Anna. "I have one other gift for you."

Anna was all ears but was waiting for the other shoe to drop.

"I can make you stronger and faster than you are now. Far more lethal should you find yourself in a battle with magic-wielding opponents. But I can only do this by accelerating your gargoyle metamorphosis."

A spike of adrenaline coursed through her blood and sent her heart pounding. Sure, she'd do anything to save the kid, but become the full package? She'd never get to live a normal life again. Oh, she knew it wasn't likely as it was, but full gargoyle? Any hope of a normal life would be gone.

If she didn't, her chances of rescuing Shadowlight were less. And she knew she would need every advantage once behind enemy lines.

She fisted her hands but met Daryna's gaze. "Fine. Do what you have to."

"Good. The process will still take some time before you complete your transformation; a few months, instead of a few years. However, within hours you'll have increased stamina and heightened senses and resistance to magic, among other advantages."

Anna nodded at the other woman's words. "So, I'll be a gargoyle sooner or later. Might as well be sooner, then."

With a nod, Daryna rested her hands on Anna's shoulders. A power that managed to be both hot and cold at the same time raced over her body, and if she'd been standing, she would have been dropped to her knees.

Nice gift, Anna thought as darkness flitted at the edges of her vision.

After what felt like half an eternity, Daryna lifted her hands away. Anna slumped sideways but managed to keep herself on the tree trunk. Her sight slowly returned and so too did her strength. All-in-all, she'd didn't feel as bad as she thought.

"Go," Daryna said. "I've done what I can to strengthen you for this task. Gather what weapons you think you will need and meet me back here in an hour. The transportation portal spell will be ready."

Anna nodded and then forced herself up off the tree trunk. Her first few steps were ungainly, but after a dozen, her body remembered how to run. Twenty steps after that, a new strength awoke within her body.

CHAPTER TWENTY-SEVEN

*B*ack at HQ, Anna darted through the temporary military base, her passage unseen. Shadow magic flickered around her form. Thanks to Gregory's training lessons, she'd mastered the concealment spell enough to fool the humans and Fae she passed. And thanks to Daryna's help, Anna was now stronger in both body and magic.

She'd covered the ground between here and where the Sorceress waited in under eight minutes, an unheard-of record time for her.

Although her new magic wasn't quite so advanced in comparison. During an earlier near-miss with a dire wolf out hunting in the forest had proved that her mastery of shadow magic wasn't yet good enough to hide her scent.

That wasn't a concern with humans. But some members of the Fae, like a dire wolf, unicorn, or pooka possessed a more advanced sense of smell. So, she went to some trouble to avoid those particular species.

It made her task harder but was also a good test considering her ultimate goal was to invade the domain of the Battle Goddess.

Getting over the fence and into headquarters was easy. Getting into the buildings—not so much. She had to wait for personnel to enter the building she wanted. This time her target was a repurposed high school. It was summer, and the military had taken over this building since it was located in close proximity to the community center.

Thankfully the scientists were working in shifts or pulling all-nighters. It wasn't terribly long before one of the scientists exited the building for a smoke break.

She walked between the sentinels on watch and slipped through the door before it closed. Inside, she stepped with care, not wanting her footfalls to give her presence away.

Making her slow, careful way by the soldiers stationed at the entrance, she traveled deeper into the building, down two flights of stairs and along the darkened hall and passed the labs. She paused and peered in a small window. Inside the classroom that had once been one of the high school's labs, lights were still on and a few whitecoats moved around.

Anna stepped away from the door and continued down the hall. The next room was where the day's batch of ward-spelled prototype weapons were stored before being field-tested. Once that was done, they'd be moved to the armory.

There were too many eyes on the armory to get inside

easily, so she'd hoped that this room would be an easier target. Which it was, but there were still problems. Like the three soldiers on guard duty she'd already walked past in the hall.

Getting her ass riddled with bullets wouldn't help Shadowlight one bit. With a glower at the nearest guard, Anna moved away from the door she wanted and headed to the end of the hall. Glancing down its length, she took in the scene.

Yep. More guards like she'd expected.

She studied them a moment, and when one turned his back and started to walk away from his buddy, Anna summoned her shadow magic and sent it out to surround him. After casting a quick glance over her shoulder and noting the other soldier was still walking in the opposite direction, Anna reached out to her target and pressed her fingers against his hand.

He jerked at the touch but dropped like a sack of bricks the next moment. She eased him to the ground and glanced up at the other target.

The second soldier turned back in her direction and was scanning the area where his buddy should have been.

"Hendricks. Peterson. Come in."

"Peterson here."

"Vickers with you?"

"Nope."

"Then we have a problem." His gun pointed unwaveringly at the spot Anna had just been.

She continued toward the next target as he scanned the hall. When she was even with him, she brushed her fingers along his jaw. It was the easiest bit of exposed skin to make contact with.

Like the first soldier, this one's eyes rolled back in his head and he went limp. She lowered him to the ground and returned to the north corridor.

The other two soldiers each felt the briefest ghostly touch and then they too were no longer a problem.

Anna returned to the door she needed and reached for the handle. It was locked which wasn't a surprise. Nor was it a problem for her increased gargoyle strength and her shadow magic.

Her magic flowed inside the lock and hardened into tiny shards of darkness which expanded within the lock mechanism. With a sharp cracking sound and the crunch of metal, the knob came off in her hand. With a bit more wiggling, the locking mechanism inside suffered a similar fate.

She stepped inside the room and saw what she needed stacked up in their storage racks.

Jackpot.

nna was exiting the building just as Major Resnick entered, trailed by an entourage. Seeing Resnick caused a stab of pain to twist deep in her guts. He'd be disappointed in her, which would hurt worse than the court-martial she knew was coming her way if she survived her self-appointed mission.

Resnick and her father were friends. She'd known him since she was a kid. Hell, he was like an uncle to her. Disappointing him was going to be far worse than the court-martial, but it couldn't be helped. Not this time.

Squaring her shoulders, she waited for Resnick and the others to file past before she darted through the closing door and out into the night. Once she was free of the base, and no longer had to be as careful of her passage, she hauled ass back to where Daryna had said to meet.

Daryna had told Anna she had an hour to gather what

she would need. She'd made it back with eleven minutes to spare. Daryna was already there and waiting.

So far, so good. While Anna wasn't certain of the other woman's real motives, she didn't have the luxury to care. Rescuing Shadowlight came first.

While she sprinted up to the spot where Daryna was working, Anna studied the area. It was greatly changed. Daryna had been busy as promised and was presently finishing up some fancy-looking spell.

To Anna's enhanced gargoyle vision, the twenty-foot circle that surrounded Daryna glowed a bluish white. It was so bright it destroyed Anna's night vision, and she had to blink away the phantom lines and spots from her vision.

"Good, you're back. I'm just finishing the last layer of the portal spell." Daryna painted two more symbols in the air with precise gestures of her hands.

After another buzzing wave of magic tingled along Anna's skin, Daryna rotated the symbols until they were hovering parallel to the ground. With a gentle push, she sent the last two symbols floating down to join the rest of the circle. Like pieces of a puzzle, they snapped into place and the entire circle glowed even brighter.

"It's ready. Come."

Anna hesitated a moment, not wanting to come so close to the vast power she felt throbbing in the glowing lines of the spell. The magic felt wild and pent-up, ready to lash out at anyone foolish enough to set order to its chaos.

After eyeing the spell for a moment more, she stepped over the first bright line.

Inside several more symbols glowed white with their

own power. Again she hesitated, but not because she was scared. She just didn't want to screw the spell up and waste time while it was fixed.

"You can walk through the magic without harm," Daryna said as she tweaked one of the symbols.

Anna shrugged and marched straight to the center of the circle. She already had all her gear packed away. She'd even taken a tranquilizer rifle. It wouldn't do any good against armor-clad enemies, but she hoped that within the heart of the Battle Goddess's domain, not everyone she encountered would be dressed in full body armor. She'd also brought three of the spell-warded rifles and enough ammo for a small siege, just in case they were fanatical enough to go in full body armor all the time.

"My spell will deliver you deep inside the Battle Goddess's territory. I designed it to have a minimal disturbance on the flows of magic in the surrounding area. So, the spell won't betray your location, but that doesn't mean your arrival won't be witnessed." Daryna shrugged in an offhanded way.

"I might pop into existence in front of a hostile. Better have my shit together. Got it. What else can I expect?"

"I've created the promised map in more detail."

Daryna held out the nondescript brown tube. Anna pulled off one end and tipped out the map. When she unrolled it, she found a hand drawn map or one created by magic. The parchment might have been honest-to-god animal skin.

But the map was legible with what looked like mountains, valleys, lakes and rivers marked out upon it.

"If something happens to the medallions, but you're not so desperate as to seek out Lord Death, show Shadowlight this map. He will be able to use his father's memories and this map to lead you safely into the neighboring kingdom of Falconsmead. It's a land ruled by Whitethorn's distant kin." Daryna paused and glanced north as if there was something there drawing away her attention.

With a shake of her head, she continued. "A warning though, they are not friendly to those who serve the Battle Goddess. Though, they do respect gargoyles. While sidhe of the Magic Realm will be suspicious of you, they will not kill you outright. But there are pookas which hunt the lands between the two kingdoms. Beware to avoid their notice."

Ah, fantasyland just sounded so delightful. "Eh, yeah. But either you, Lillian or Gregory will come for Shadowlight and me eventually, right?"

"Never fear. You both still have a part to play in this before it is over."

Anna narrowed her eyes. That sounded a lot like demigods moving pieces on the chessboard again. Well, fortunately, she was a knight with really sharp claws, big-ass guns, and enough ordnance to make her enemies bleed.

Daryna walked from the glowing circle as she continued to instruct Anna. "The spell will drop you about a day's walk from the Battle Goddess's temple. With the map to guide you, you will find the temple easily enough. However, the time of day you arrive will influence your plans."

Anna stopped herself from strumming her fingers

against her thigh. Obviously, she wasn't going to attempt a rescue in broad daylight.

"Your instincts will be to try to infiltrate the temple at night, but that would be a mistake. Many of the creatures that serve her are nocturnal and will be hibernating during the day, or if awake, their senses dulled."

"Like vampires?"

"Worse, my dear. Much worse."

"Nice," Anna muttered to herself. "But the ward-spelled weapons should still work on them?"

"Yes. But your best defense will be secrecy and shadows. Don't let your guard down for a moment, even in the daytime. Not all who serve her are night dwellers."

"I won't," Anna agreed. *I like my own ass, thanks. And I won't do Shadowlight a scrap of good if I'm dead.*

"Do you have any other questions?"

"Hell, yes. But we're out of time. Let's do this before Gregory finds us."

"Very well."

Daryna stepped from the circle and raised her arms. As she did so, the circle's light flickered and shifted to shades of pastel. When she began to chant, the pale color shifted again, changing to a darker hue, fiercer and somehow more aggressive in tone. Again, Anna was reminded of the wildness she sensed in the magic.

"May the Divine Ones continue to bless you."

Bless me? Not bloody likely. Let me survive with my skin intact to torture me more later? Hopefully.

A wall of power encircled her, and a great pressure descended upon her body. It continued to increase. There was a reason she hadn't joined the air force. Pulling G's wasn't her idea of fun. For a moment, she thought the magic was going to grind her bones into the ground.

Above her, the magic swirled in a violent vortex. Her heart in her throat, she watched as what she was certain was an angry and ravenous wormhole reached down and swallowed her whole.

Gravity vanished along with any sense of up or down. As Anna's body was catapulted into the next realm over, she wished she'd thought to ask more about the transportation spell. Like what to expect and how bloody long would it last?

At least, she could take some pride in the fact that she wasn't screaming or puking.

Then as swiftly as the sensory bombardment had started, it abruptly ended.

Her head still spinning, Anna found herself on her hands and knees in a stream. It was icy cold and flowed down a steep slope before it eventually reached the valley floor a few hundred feet below.

Anna picked herself up out of the stream and looked around in more detail. The valley seemed uninhabited, and so far as she could tell no one had seen her arrival. She stomped ashore after she had determined moving wasn't going to draw unwanted attention.

"Welcome to fantasyland. Methinks it's going to go downhill from here."

She glanced at the sun to gauge how much daylight she had left only to find a second, smaller one riding in the sky with it.

Two suns.

Yep.

Shaking her head in disbelief, she called her shadow magic to hide and then headed for the closest trees to act as cover. Once she oriented herself using the map, she would start the hunt for Shadowlight. Now that she was here in this realm, the tiny speck of magic that burned deep in her brain detected Shadowlight faint and far away. But alive.

Never had she been so happy for her magic. She only hoped he could sense her and know help was on its way.

"I'm coming for you, kid. Just hang on."

CHAPTER TWENTY-NINE

Daryna turned her back on the fading ring of magic she'd used to send Anna to the Magic Realm. Knowing her time was limited, she immediately began summoning another spell that would carry her to Gryton's camp. If he was still there. Weariness was creeping across her senses, and she knew her body was beginning to show the stress of calling upon so much magic in so short a time. But it couldn't be helped. And she still had more spell work to complete this night.

With a focused push of her will, a portal spell appeared in the air. Daryna raised her chin and prepared to face her son. Between one step and the next, she was far from where she'd been.

Here the air was free of the stink of humans and technology. The rich scent of balsam fir and other evergreens filled her lungs. She breathed deep and wiggled her bare toes in the needles and loam under her feet.

Being born into a dryad body had some interesting advantages. The trees told her all that went on in their domain. Gryton had returned less than two hours ago, but he'd already set a few defensive spells before limping into his temporary home.

Relief that he was still here washed through her.

If he'd intentionally betrayed her and deliberately orchestrated Shadowlight's capture, Gryton wouldn't have returned to the first place she'd look. No son of hers would be so foolish.

In truth, she hadn't assumed Gryton had betrayed her. While his earlier thoughts had been tainted with distrust of her motives, there had been no dishonesty. It was good that she wouldn't have to hunt him down and start fresh with his taming.

Expanding her power, she learned more about his condition. Presently, his emotions came to her. He was awake and in pain and expecting to be hunted down at any moment, but his honor demanded he take responsibility for his own failures.

During the fight, Gregory had injured him, but she hadn't known how badly.

"Gryton, my child. Lower the defenses, I'm coming in."

"I'm not a child," came his surly reply. "Even though I was foolishly naïve to believe I could trick the Battle Goddess and the warriors under my command, I didn't intentionally betray you or the young gargoyle."

"I know." Daryna grinned. If he was grumpy, his injuries couldn't have been too extensive.

Gryton didn't lower his defenses as she'd asked, but

they became visible without her having to counter them. She carefully picked her way over and around all the trigger spells.

She ducked her head as she stepped through the cavern's low entrance. Inside was the familiar narrow crevice that finally widened several paces in. Firelight flickered on the walls, but there was nothing cooking over the fire.

Gryton sat next to it. His upper body armor was missing, and he was working on healing a dozen shallow slashes that covered his shoulders, arms, and chest. The damage allowed his internal fire magic to glow from behind the injuries.

Not that he would carry them for long. She planned to aid in healing him well before the dawn when Gregory would begin his hunt.

"Lillian did an excellent job on you."

Gryton snorted. His lips curled away from his fangs, but there was a hint of admiration. "See how well you do going into battle and trying to overpower your opponents without actually killing them. And when your opponents are gargoyles, let me assure you that is no easy task."

"Yes, about that," Daryna said as she set her bag of supplies down next to Gryton. "Gregory has enough of your blood and essence to track you. He's attending to Lillian's minor injuries, but once he has done that, he will be on the hunt well before dawn, I imagine."

Gryton ran a finger along one of the slashes as he murmured a healing chant. "I'm not going to sit by and allow my gargoyle sire to kill me without a fight."

"I don't intend for you and Gregory to meet face-to-face just yet. He's not ready to hear the truth." Daryna reached out and placed a hand over one of Gryton's wounds and healed it. "I intend to weave a spell upon you that will hide you from Gregory's searching magic. It's not a permanent fix, but it will be better than nothing."

Again, Gryton grunted in way of acknowledgment.

"You're very like your father. Grumpy. Non-communicative. Brooding..."

His fangs flashed again. "What does it matter if I am? He'll still hate me on principle."

That might very well be true, Daryna decided. But she didn't utter that aloud.

"We have other problems."

He jerked his head in a swift affirmative, his expression turning slightly less haughty. "I only expected those I specified for the mission to come. That many more came must mean the Battle Goddess suspects me of treason."

"Perhaps she did, but those who captured Shadowlight saw Gregory attack you. They will carry that news back to the Battle Goddess. If we are lucky, she will assume you are actually innocent of betrayal and that by coming here you acted to retrieve the collars that Darkness and River stole. And your actions also allowed Shadowlight to be captured. We can use that to our advantage. It never hurts to have a spy in our enemy's court."

"That wasn't my intention. If I go back, she will see through my deception and will seek my death just as surely as her brother did in the past."

Daryna laughed. "Then tonight's session will be about

how to hide your innermost thoughts, showing her only what you want her to see, what she will think she has pried from your unwilling mind."

Gryton glanced down at the fire so his pale skin didn't betray his shame. "I lack the control needed to do as you say."

"As a child raised in her kingdom for eight years, under her ever-watchful eye, I managed to hide my plans from her," Daryna said as she handed him another piece of white gauze. "If I could do that for all those years, you'll be able to manage well enough with some guidance from me. You've already excelled well beyond what you were capable of a few days ago."

Gryton still looked skeptical but seemed willing to put his trust in her. "Very well. You haven't misled me. But I still don't know if I'll be able to rescue Shadowlight from the Battle Goddess's domain."

"Oh. You won't need to worry about that. I've already sent another for that purpose."

"You sent Gregory, after all? I thought you said he was attending to Lillian."

"Oh, he has a plan to rescue Shadowlight. It involves sinking his claws into you, but I came up with a better, less risky idea about how to extract the young gargoyle cub from our enemy."

One of Gryton's eyebrows arched in question.

Ah, she'd surprised him. It only lasted a moment before his expression smoothed into understanding. "You've sent the berserker. But why? She is nowhere near ready to undertake her part in your plan. Her hope of successfully freeing Shadowlight is far less than my own odds."

"My son, you have so much to learn. This is a long game. I don't expect the hybrid to succeed. Not right away. First, she needs to see what true evil is. She needs to focus all that potential she has locked inside her. Only then will we be able to shape her into a weapon to aim at the heart of the Battle Goddess."

Gryton looked unhappy. "If she goes after Shadowlight, she will become the Battle Goddess's weapon as well, not yours."

"Like you are?"

"That's different."

"Not so very much. And, yes, the Battle Goddess will teach her hate. But the human is a rare soul. Her moral code is an iron core that runs deep. The Battle Goddess will not be able to corrupt her. Besides, Shadowlight will need a friend in the unfortunate situation he has found himself in. The shared hardship will only cement their bond of friendship into something truly astounding."

"How can you be so confident the human hybrid will survive with her morals intact?"

"Because," Daryna said with absolute certainty that came from far outside her own mind. "Shadowlight finding and saving Anna was Divine will."

Gryton laughed, a harsh sound full of bitter amusement. "It must be true. Only the Divine Ones would create such a harrowing and complex path to inflict upon some hapless soul."

"The Divine Ones set many tests and trials so that our souls may learn and grow."

"Then I must be very well learned."

"Indeed," Daryna said. "However, there is still much you must learn, and time is short. I still need to heal you, weave a few spells, and then go seek out Lillian and Gregory. All before they realize I'm missing."

"Life is never dull, is it Mother?"

"No, my son," Daryna said with genuine mirth. "It never is. Now let me teach you how to lie so that even the Battle Goddess won't know the truth from falsehood."

CHAPTER THIRTY

A pounding on the door jolted Lillian out of deep sleep. Gregory growled out something dark and menacing, which was quite a feat since he was in human form. But that didn't impede his reflexes at all. He was already fully awake and stalking buck-naked toward the door.

"Gregory. For the love of God, put clothes on."

Of course he ignored her.

Lillian grabbed her own robe and pulled it on moments before Gregory jerked the door open. "Are the Lord of the Underworld and the Lady of Battles presently battling on the front lawn?"

Gran stood framed by the door. Major Resnick was at her shoulder and looking downright impatient. Lillian's grandmother answered first, her voice sounding a touch distracted as she took in Gregory's form. "No. I don't think so, my boy. Something else has come up though."

Lillian was bringing Gregory a robe to wear when Major Resnick pushed past him like he wasn't afraid of getting bounced back out into the hall by an angry, naked human-formed gargoyle.

"Anna is missing. Do you know anything about it?"

Each word came out clipped and barely controlled. It was completely unlike the Resnick she had gotten to know. Gregory must have sensed it as well, for he merely took the robe Lillian offered and answered truthfully. "No. We haven't seen Anna since she left with you after Shadowlight was taken. I wasn't aware she was missing."

Lillian stepped in closer. "Anna was really broken up about what happened to Shadowlight. Are you sure she hasn't gone someplace to be alone? She might be out in the forest hunting."

Resnick snorted. "Oh, I'm pretty sure she's out hunting, but it's not deer. We have security footage of her going into the restricted area, attacking fellow soldiers, and then stealing an assortment of the modified assault rifles and side arms."

"You're certain it was Anna?" Gregory asked. "Several species of Fae can shapeshift and make themselves look like someone else."

"I remember. Like you did when you pretended to be one of my men." Resnick shook his head. "Unfortunately, no, I don't think that's what happened. Anna was clearly using shadow magic." Resnick tripped over the word magic like he was still having trouble using the term. "Only a gargoyle has that ability, correct?"

"Yes," Gregory agreed.

"The only reason we know it was her is that we just had the banshee ward-spell the surveillance cameras to better protect the compound."

"Give me a few moments and I'll be able to confirm if it was Anna and not a shapeshifter," Gregory said as he closed his eyes and summoned magic.

The beginnings of a spell raised gooseflesh upon Lillian's arms. After a moment, he huffed angrily. "There are only two gargoyles in the Mortal Realm. Lillian and me."

Lillian jerked in surprise. "You're saying Anna is gone. Do you think Gryton got to her like he did Whitethorn and Goswin?"

"I don't know, but I intend to find out." Gregory growled. "Take me to the place where Anna trespassed. I should be able to pick up her scent and then determine if she was forced into doing this."

Resnick nodded. "If Gryton didn't get to her, then I fear she's gone after him on her own to take revenge for what happened to Shadowlight. She might even now be Gryton's prisoner."

"I wouldn't be so certain of that," Gregory said, closing his eyes. A moment later, Lillian felt him call power as he shifted back to his gargoyle form.

She stared at Gregory, but it wasn't because he'd shifted. She was getting better at reading his thoughts. "My God. You think Anna has gone after Shadowlight. But how is that even possible. She doesn't have the power or knowledge to get to the Magic Realm. You once said that traveling between the realms took a lot of magical strength."

"Yes, it does. And, no, Anna couldn't get there on her own. But if she had help..."

The Mother's Sorceress.

Gregory thought Anna had somehow convinced Daryna to help. Lillian was worried for Anna, of course, but she couldn't bring herself to regret the woman's decision. If Anna had managed to convince the Sorceress to help, it meant that Daryna thought Anna had a chance of rescuing Shadowlight.

Resnick tilted his head to look up at Gregory. "There's only one problem. Anna would never go against orders."

Gregory's tail lashed back and forth with a great deal of violence. When Lillian touched his thoughts, she felt his ongoing internal debate. He was thinking about sharing something with Resnick he'd rather not.

At last Gregory sighed and drew in a deep breath. "There is something we have not shared with you or your superiors. It regards Anna and Shadowlight and how the young gargoyle managed to save Anna's life. It wasn't natural; not even for a gargoyle."

Resnick froze in place, waiting for Gregory to continue.

"Shadowlight was altered by the Battle Goddess. One such change is his ability to use his blood to heal others. Although, it doesn't just heal them; it changes them as it did Anna. That part you know. What you don't know is that there is a magical component that binds them together. Anna is Shadowlight's second."

"Second?"

"Second in Command," Gregory clarified. "If fate had not intervened, Shadowlight would have grown up to lead the Battle Goddess's armies, but he would also possess the ability to convert others and enslave them. Anna is already soul-bound to him. That bond will only grow stronger as he ages. Already her need to save him is affecting her thinking. It's a mindless need to protect. One that I don't know if Anna can fight."

Lillian, still linked to Gregory's thoughts, sorted through them for the one answer she still wanted.

If Anna couldn't reach Shadowlight on her own, would she seek out someone else who could?

Gregory's thoughts were darkening and becoming more upset, but he did share them. "There are very few beings with the strength to travel between the realms. Presently, there are only three here in the Mortal Realm—myself, my Sorceress, and Commander Gryton."

Either Anna had gone hunting Gryton and had been captured and taken prisoner. Or Daryna had helped Anna reach the Magic Realm.

Daryna was a much better alternative to hope for than Gryton, but Lillian didn't know what would have changed the Sorceress's mind. She'd been most adamant that it was too dangerous for either herself or Gregory. If it was too hazardous to the Avatars, what possible chance did Anna have?

Resnick's expression told them that Gregory's comment had clarified some conclusion he'd already come to. "Then we can only assume she went after Commander Gryton and he was waiting for such a move and has already captured and transported her like the cub."

"That is the greatest likelihood." With a deeply

unhappy growl, Gregory continued. "I will track Anna's trail and get to the bottom of this. As soon as I know what is truly afoot, I will pass the information along to you."

Major Resnick nodded sharply. "I'll brief my superiors."

After the military man had left with Gran in tow, Lillian turned to Gregory and asked the other question in her mind that he didn't want to face.

"Do you know where Daryna is?"

"No," Gregory said with horror and disbelief in his voice. "And I cannot sense her anywhere near. She has hidden her presence from me. But I will find her."

And by his tone, Daryna was in for a world of trouble when he did.

"Then it's possible she's been working with Gryton all along. I'm coming with you."

"No. The child. It's too dangerous."

"I'm pregnant. Not dying. And no, I don't want to risk our child, but I must go. If Daryna has been playing with us all along," which Lillian thought was entirely the truth, "then I can't trust you to deal with her. I'll make the hard decision. You can't. Killing her would destroy a part of you."

"Lillian," Gregory said in a gruff voice edged with pain. "You are no match for her. Besides, we don't know that she's tainted. It's possible that the amount of magic she's called upon today has hastened her body's degradation. Thus, her mind and judgment may be impaired. If so, I will do what I can to help heal the damage."

"You don't know that though."

"No. That's why you can't come."

"That's why I am coming, you great overprotective idiot. I am the one being in all the realms she won't kill. She needs my body, so the soul and power of the Mother's Sorceress will have a home to return to. And she wants this child." Lillian rested her hands on her belly. "She's wanted to have your child for a very long time. Anyone can see that."

Gregory glanced down at his talons. "And I have wanted to grant her that wish for many lifetimes. It has been my great, secret shame. Even the thought is a betrayal of my vows to the Divine Ones."

"Gregory, they are the ones at fault. Wishing to have a child with the one you love should never be a sin."

"A part of me agrees with you, but that changes nothing."

"Fine. You're unreasonable, but so too am I. This is the last time I say this. I am going. Now let's go see what has become of Anna and if it's Gryton or Daryna who is at fault."

Gregory was slow to nod agreement, but eventually, he did. Smart male.

It wasn't until he started for the door that she noticed that he was clothed, and his arm and wrist bands were back in place. However, she was still naked under her robe. "Hold up. I need to shift and then dress."

He halted with his hand on the door but nodded and waited patiently for her to shapeshift into her gargoyle form and dress. Then, together, they headed down to the front drive where Resnick was waiting with a small convoy of armored vehicles.

CHAPTER THIRTY-ONE

Gregory had allowed himself to be crammed into one of the vehicles with Lillian. There really wasn't room for one gargoyle, let alone two. But Resnick had insisted.

And he'd learned when to pick his battles in a long-ago lifetime.

They arrived at the military headquarters a short time later, and he and Lillian were escorted inside. Already, he'd caught a hint of Anna's trail. Her scent was the same as he remembered. There was no hint of either Gryton or Daryna. So, Anna had been by herself, at least at this point.

Gregory continued deeper into the building where the weapons were stored just to be certain. But again, he found nothing unusual in her scent. He followed the trail back to the surface and on outside, north and west away from the military's base.

Anna had continued out of town and into the forest. Resnick and his team were still following him, but they were having a more difficult time in the forest.

Gregory continued at a fast run. About twenty minutes outside of town, he found a clearing in the forest where a great weaving had been created.

The spell had already unraveled, the energy dissipating back into the surrounding land. But he would recognize the essence of that power anywhere. It was the match to his own.

"Daryna was here a short time ago. Maybe four hours ago at most. This was a spell woven with the purpose of transporting Anna to the Magic Realm. I can see that much from what remains of the spell."

"It was not Gryton then?"

Gregory felt his ears pin to his head and his wings clamp tight to his back. "I wouldn't be so sure. Afterward, Daryna traveled from this location to another north of here."

Lillian's expression and body language mirrored his own, and he knew that as much as she didn't like Daryna, she'd truly hoped for his sake her suspicions were wrong.

"Do we follow? Or do you want to gather more of our Fae allies?" Lillian asked.

"We'll go alone. There's nothing the Fae can do that won't get them killed."

Looking uncertain, Lillian nodded.

Gregory wrapped one wing around her shoulders. "I must first prepare some battle spells. It would be better here than later when danger might be coming at us from an unknown direction. We do not yet know for certain if Gryton is involved with this, but I can't rule out that he somehow enslaved Daryna."

Even as he said the words, he didn't know how they could be true. Daryna was too powerful to be enslaved by one such as Gryton.

After Gregory had woven several spells of protection to cocoon her body in an invisible force, Lillian had sat a little way away with her tail curled around her legs and her wings folded tight to her back while Gregory finished preparing other, deadlier spells. When he at last called her back to his side, she went. Together, they would face whatever they would find on the other side of the portal. She passed through the portal spell and experienced the strange sensation of having the ground shift underneath her feet. After a few queasy seconds, Lillian found herself in an unknown forest. The trees here were different. When Lillian started forward, Gregory forestalled her.

"Traps."

Lillian nodded in understanding. Her dryad blood tuned into the trees around her and she realized they were whispering to her. They spoke of a hard-minded fire elemental who had bled upon the ground and burned their roots with his heat.

'Gryton is here,' Lillian whispered into Gregory's mind.

'I know. I can smell his blood, but not sense him at all. The Mother's Sorceress has been weaving a spell of protection around him.'

Lillian was still mulling over that bit of news when Gregory pointed out a narrow crevice in the bedrock wall that rose up out of the ground in front of them. The land here was rockier, the bones of the earth showing through more readily.

Venturing into a cave was always a bad idea as far as Lillian was concerned.

As he moved slowly forward, Lillian followed, her swords held at the ready. She could feel where Gregory's spells of protection hummed along her body, tingling with an unpleasant itch. However, the mild discomfort was well worth it if those same spells could protect her and her child from danger. While she knew she had to be here—that knowledge anchored deep in her being—that didn't mean she wanted to go into that cave.

But she entered anyway, ducking to avoid scraping her horns on the low ceiling. Ahead, she could see the dim flickering of fire against the tunnel walls.

Had she not been so focused on the dangers of the traps and what other surprises might be waiting for them in the cave, she would have registered the scent of a campfire much sooner.

Someone planned to be here for a while if they'd gone to the trouble of building a fire.

The narrow tunnel they were following opened into a vast cavern, and Gregory straightened to his full height.

"Hello, my protector." Daryna's voice was all calm confidence as usual.

But Gregory's menacing growl spurred Lillian into pushing past the barrier of his wings. On the opposite side of the campfire, Daryna stood with one hand wrapped around Commander Gryton's arm as if physically holding him in place.

Lillian wasn't sure what she found more stunning—that Daryna could hold Gryton against his will or that Tin Man hadn't launched an attack yet.

"Gregory, wait," Daryna said, her tone beseeching him to listen. "It's not what it looks like. I haven't turned traitor. There are things you do not know. Critical information that will fill in so many blanks."

Daryna's rushed plea did nothing to sway Gregory's actions, though. Lillian could feel the cold, destructive magic flowing from the Spirit Realm, building within him as he readied to unleash the battle spells he'd forged earlier.

"I understand well enough." He released the first wave of power.

It raced across the length of the cavern to slam into a shield that encircled Daryna and Gryton. That didn't deter Gregory in the slightest, and he launched another blast of power upon them.

Again and again, he struck, the magic swirling in wild currents around the cave. It beat at the walls, floor, and ceiling, seeking a way free. But it seemed unable to escape past Gregory's wings where he blocked the entrance.

"Gregory, stop," Daryna ordered. "I command you."

"You are not my Sorceress. Shout all you want. I'll not obey this time." His voice dropped to a growl.

"Let me fight," Gryton yelled at Daryna. "Or your gargoyle half is going to kill me long before he listens to you."

Daryna shook her head stubbornly. "No! Gregory listen. Gryton is needed. He is important. With his help, we can overthrow the Battle Goddess."

"You are delusional," Gregory hissed.

Daryna raised her hand higher, bracing herself as Gregory tossed more power at her. "My gargoyle, don't make me hurt you."

Gregory snorted. "Surrender and let me deal with Gryton and then we will talk. You are either tainted, influenced by him, or your judgment is impaired because of damage to your mind and body."

"It's not any of those reasons. Let me explain."

Gregory snarled. "You can explain after I've killed Gryton."

Lillian's lungs strained to draw in air as the pressure continued to build within the cavern. Knowing the danger of a collapse was a very real possibility, Lillian whispered in Gregory's mind. *'You're going to bury all of us under a few tons of rock if you keep this up.'*

'At least they'd be trapped.'

'Did you miss the 'us' part?'

Huffing, he tilted his head enough to meet her gaze. *'I have reinforced our escape route; however, Daryna and Gryton will not be so lucky.'*

Lillian studied Gryton and Daryna with some misgiving. Gryton wasn't fighting. Perhaps the Mother's Sorceress did know something Gregory didn't. And hadn't the original plan been to trap and milk Gryton for information, so they could use him to help free Shadowlight?

Well, Gryton was right there. Cornered, if not yet captured.

As if sensing her regard, he shifted his gaze to study her.

He raised his visor, and she met his dark, almond-shaped eyes. They were familiar. It took her a moment and then she had it. His intense brown eyes reminded her of Gregory's when he was in his human form.

Above their heads, sharp snaps echoed from the tortured ceiling. A wide crack now stretched across the rocky surface. A second fissure opening made Lillian's sensitive ears quiver. A moment later, half the ceiling was falling toward Daryna.

Gryton reacted faster, throwing himself over Daryna, shielding her smaller body from the pieces his power failed to vaporize in time. The cavern filled with a potent mix of dust, steam, and heat.

Even the added protections Gregory had woven around Lillian didn't block it all.

Coughing, she backed out of the tunnel and into fresh air. Once she had her breath back, she stooped down to go back in. Before she'd made it a step, an explosive shock-wave raced outward from somewhere deep in the cave.

Gregory was tossed free of the tunnel and rolled a couple of times before he sprang back to his feet. Gryton was the next out of the tunnel, Daryna close at his heels.

However, the Sorceress wasn't fast enough to catch the Commander.

"You will not harm my mother!"

The bellowed words shocked Lillian. And apparently Gregory, too. He'd been in a threatening crouch, about to launch another attack, but Gryton's words had the big gargoyle slowly standing up.

While his magic was still raging around him, he looked beyond his opponent to meet Daryna's eyes.

"You must not harm Gryton," Daryna screamed, calling more of her own magic.

Gryton didn't seem to have the same concerns for Gregory and drew his sword. Swinging it in a wide arc, he aimed for the gargoyle's abdomen.

Gregory held out a hand, one that glowed brightly with power. Gryton's strike was deflected, but the armor-clad warrior recovered quickly. Dancing out of the range of Gregory's counter attack, Gryton moved to strike again.

Lillian was still struck on Gryton's earlier cry.

Mother?

His familiar eyes.

Gregory's eyes.

Oh, God.

It was impossible. Yet when she glanced at Daryna, she knew.

Their soul link flared to life and the other woman's thoughts were suddenly in Lillian's mind. *Gryton is ours. The first born between us.'*

Gregory was the father. Daryna was the mother. That

could only mean in some past life they had broken their most sacred vows.

Here was a monster that the Avatars had birthed into the universe against Divine will.

But why didn't Gregory remember?

Gryton came at Gregory again. The gargoyle snapped out a hand and closed his fingers around the shorter male's throat, his talons digging in. He hoisted Gryton off the ground and then reached out with his other hand and pried Gryton's helmet from his head. Gregory's muzzle dipped closer and dragged in a deep lungful of air.

His expression shifting between shock and disbelief, he just stood there holding Gryton off the ground. The other male twisted and freed a knife from a sheath at his waist and lashed out, aiming for a soft target.

Gregory blocked the strike and shook the other male like he was a dusty rag. However, the gargoyle had not killed the other male yet, so clearly, he was uncertain.

Hell, Lillian was uncertain, too.

Was Gryton really their son? One raised by the Battle Goddess?

Gryton must've sensed Gregory's reluctance as well, for he struck with his knife again. This time finding flesh. It was a demon blade, Lillian realized.

With a snarl of pain, Gregory jerked the blade from his bicep and called more spirit magic. The demon blade loosed a screech and then vaporized a moment later. The distraction had been enough to allow Gryton to gain his freedom.

Gregory called more power. Was that added strength intended for capturing or killing Gryton, Lillian wondered?

Daryna must have had similar doubts, for a great weaving began to form in the air directly in front of her. By the intensity of the bright coloration flickering at its core Lillian knew it was going to be big and badass. One capable of doing severe damage to its target.

"Stop." At her shout three pairs of eyes locked on her.

Lillian squared her shoulders, drew in a deep breath, and then stalked forward until she was standing in the center of a triangle, each opponent making one of the points.

"We need to talk this out."

When no one responded, Lillian tried a different tactic. "All the realms lose if the Avatars go to war against each other."

That got a grunt from Gregory, and after a moment, Daryna closed her hand on her own spell.

Two down.

Lillian looked to Gryton next. He was standing slightly further away than the other two, but Lillian could still easily feel his potent magic.

She studied him unhappily. While he might be her son, he was also a mass murderer. But even so, she did not want to see him killed by Gregory. She told herself it was because she didn't want Gregory to suffer from the knowledge that he'd killed his own son.

"Daryna, you said Gryton is our son—that's why you stopped me from killing him back in the glade when you were still a hamadryad and I had him under my sword. I understand now why you did what you did. But it doesn't make it right."

Lillian turned her attention entirely upon Gryton. Now that she was looking, she could see greater family resemblance between father and son. There was something similar in the way they carried themselves, the grace with which they moved.

"Whose side are you on?" Lillian asked.

"My own," Gryton said with stark honesty. "I have never had anyone else to rely upon. Since it doesn't seem like my sire will be harming my mother in the immediate future, I think I'll pass on the other family activities you have planned."

Faster than anyone could stop him, he darted sideways and dove into a portal spell Lillian only noticed now. Between blinks, there was a flash of magic and he was gone. Gregory growled and then charged the spot where Gryton had been, but Lillian intercepted him before he could give chase.

"Gregory, you will not go after Gryton. Later you can, but first, we need to talk to Daryna." While she'd said 'talk' she actually meant interrogate.

He snarled again, but instead of following Gryton like he so clearly wanted to, he came over to Lillian.

She held out her hand and he took it. Together they walked over to face Daryna. To say Gregory was calmer would be a lie, but at least he seemed rational again. "Were you able to verify that Gryton is our son, like he and Daryna claim?"

The answer to that question would affect what they did

from this point forward. She could feel the tension in his fingers that ran on up his arms. His entire body was rigid with emotions flowing through him.

At last, he was able to spit out what kept catching in his throat. "Gryton is our son."

CHAPTER THIRTY-TWO

*E*ven as the words flowed from him, Gregory still didn't understand how this...this sacrilege had come into being. He had a son born of his other half. Forbidden, impossible, and yet somehow Gryton existed.

Gregory had no memory of the event or those that had led up to Gryton's birth. His mind kept wanting to name it all some trickery devised by the Battle Goddess.

And, yet, now that he'd reached into Gryton's mind, his essence, the facts were irrefutable.

Gryton was his son.

He collapsed to his knees. Then like it had a mind of its own, his tail coiled around his body. For the first time in his existence, the impossible had become possible. And it was more horrible than he could face.

Forsworn. He was an oath breaker. He'd betrayed his creators.

"Oh, my beloved," Daryna said as she came to stand before him. "Please look at me."

When he didn't respond, she dropped to her knees in front of him. At his back, he could feel Lillian close. Her hand came to rest on his shoulder.

But nothing was real to him at that moment.

He didn't know how long he sat there in shock, his mind working to understand his ultimate betrayal, but slowly Daryna's words invaded the chaos of his thoughts.

"I didn't know what Gryton was until he used my hamadryad tree to travel to this realm," Daryna said. "Had he known that my hamadryad was, in fact, the Mother's Sorceress at that time, I doubt Gryton would have used the tree to travel here. Whatever the case, when Gryton came, I learned what he was. Since I was a hamadryad at the time, I did not think the same way as I do now. All I knew was that Gryton was mine, my child. That's why I didn't let Lillian kill him when she had the chance."

"I knew you were up to something," Lillian said, but her tone lacked bite.

She, too, was surprised by this, Gregory realized. He tilted his head so he could brush his muzzle against her hand. Weak. He was weak to need that comfort, but he did.

"You are not weak, my gargoyle." It was Daryna speaking again.

He finally met her eyes.

"I learned more about our son while I was still a hamadryad. But it was only after I was born to this form, that I was able to truly talk to Gryton. At first, he was rather hostile, thinking that I would try to destroy him." Daryna sighed softly. "He has been hunted from the moment of his birth. Lord Death knew what Gryton was and sent every last gargoyle after him. The Lady of Battles also knew he was our son and she offered him shelter from her twin's hunters."

"Well," Lillian said, "That explains why he's a blood-thirsty mass murderer. That doesn't explain why you are helping him."

Daryna turned to Lillian. "He is our son. The life he leads was forced upon him. He had no choice."

"He didn't have to serve the Battle Goddess," Lillian countered.

"And where else would he have gone if he refused the Battle Goddess's aid?"

Gregory could hear Lillian's teeth snap together. She was silent. He reached out to her mind to find it calmer than his, but just as uncertain. She felt responsible for Gryton's actions. Gregory silently agreed with her assessment. A monster had been born into the universe because of the Avatars. That made Gryton and all he'd done their responsibility.

Somehow Gregory would have to make this right.

"How," he said at last. "How did it happen and how are we still here? The Divine Ones should have destroyed us for such a violation."

Daryna glanced down at her hands and then after a moment reached out for his.

"I don't remember the how, either. But Gryton said he had inherited some of our memories—like a father gargoyle would pass memories to his son, or a mother dryad would pass them to her daughter. But when I asked Gryton what he knew, he said he did not understand why we acted as we did. All he knew was that our coming together was not some accident. It was a deliberate choice we made."

Gregory snorted in shock. "What?"

That...that would mean they'd acted against the will of their creators purposely. It wasn't just a moment of passion that had gone too far. Which would have been bad enough. But to have willfully chosen this?

Growling, Gregory shook off their hands and stood. He could not contain the growing horror inside himself. He paced between the trees for many moments before returning and halting before the Mother's Sorceress.

"Our choice should have led to our destruction. Why are we still here?"

Lillian came to stand beside him and rested her hand on his arm. When he turned to her, she arched an eyebrow. "You make it sound like you'd rather be dead?"

Gregory sighed. "No. Of course not. But the Divine Ones should have acted to correct our...transgression."

Daryna cleared her throat. "You think they didn't? Neither of us remembers the life before this one."

Slowly Gregory glanced over his shoulder at Daryna. "Life?"

"Yes. Gryton and I compared a few memories. From what we were able to put together, I've either misplaced an entire lifetime of memories, or the Divine Ones stripped them away. I'm pretty sure I know which it is."

Gregory swallowed hard. "I still don't..."

"Here," Daryna held out her hand. "Take from my mind what I've learned while training Gryton to control his powers. It will be faster than having me try to explain it."

He hesitated a moment, not really wanting to have this new reality become even more real than it already was. It was a foolish wish, no doubt, but he still didn't want to face the truth head on.

Instead, it was Lillian who reached for Daryna's outstretched hand, his mate doing what he wasn't brave enough to do. After a few moments, Lillian released Daryna's hand with a curse.

"That was...freaking strange. But, Gregory, I think Daryna is speaking the truth. Gryton, too, in his own twisted way. At some point in the past, we chose to break our vows."

"Yes," Daryna said as she glanced down at her hands. "Gryton is our child, and while I don't know our reasoning at the time since Gryton hasn't mastered all his memories, I do know that we chose to bring him into existence. And while the Divine Ones stripped our memories from that last life, they also let us continue as we have always been. We are still their Avatars, and they sent us back to fulfill some purpose in this life."

Daryna's voice softened, but still held a note of conviction. "I believe we have been sent back this time to stop the Lady of Battles once and for all. I intend to free Gryton from her and lead him back to the Light. I think in our last life, we knew the Battle Goddess was growing bolder and that she would find a way to upset the balance and bring war to all the realms. While I can't know for certain, I do believe we birthed Gryton into the universe to be her replacement..."

"Replacement," Gregory growled and then modulated his tone. "While I would like to see the Battle Goddess forcibly returned to the Divine Ones for healing, it is not for us to go against Divine judgment. They have allowed her to remain within the Magic Realm. Thus, they must believe the Battle Goddess needs to learn the cost of her own actions."

"You don't believe that," Daryna said. "Or at least something made you set aside your beliefs at some point in our last life together."

"Even you admit that you are only going on the flawed and incomplete jumble of memories I gifted to Gryton at his conception." He paced as he mulled over this new dilemma. "It's more likely that the Divine Ones scrubbed our memories and then sent us back here as a chance to fix our mistake. A test. One last chance to prove our worthiness."

Daryna shook her head. "No. Think about it. Clearly, Lord Death called back his gargoyle army. Otherwise, there would have been a war between the twins. And only once has Lord Death ever acted without a direct command from the Divine Ones."

"Guesses."

"Yes. For now. But think about it. While our creators might not have sanctioned Gryton's birth, I think they have come to see some use for him. I would even hazard a guess that since their own Avatars went against their wishes, our creators might be thinking long and hard about their decision regarding the Lady of Battles."

"You may think that if you want," Gregory said, slowly growing calmer as new purpose filled him. He would find out what was really going on and then do whatever he must to serve the Light. But Lillian was correct. Battling his other half would not benefit anyone except the Battle Goddess. Aloud Gregory said, "But I will not come to my own conclusions without more facts. First order of business is to find Gryton and question him."

"Regardless of what you choose to believe at present, the fact remains that the Divine Ones took our memories, unmade us, and then forged us anew for a purpose. We wouldn't be here otherwise."

CHAPTER THIRTY-THREE

*L*illian had sensed when Gregory's growing despair had changed to a better mindset. If hunting down one's child was a better mindset. But for now, if he was focusing on finding a solution instead of the fact that they'd given life to a monster with unknown powers and ambiguous loyalty, Lillian was okay with that. Because it was clear the Mortal Realm would never survive a war between the Avatars.

Daryna was clearly going to protect Gryton. Equally clear was the fact that Gregory was going to do what he must to serve the Light.

Why the heck couldn't the Light clean up its own mess just this once?

Yeah. Right. That wasn't likely to happen. So that left Lillian to act as the negotiator. Then noting the dark glowers Gregory and Daryna were sending each other,

Lillian thought that maybe divorce attorney was more accurate.

"We need to come to a peaceful agreement." Lillian stepped between them to make her point. "If the Avatars go to war with each other, everyone loses. Yes?"

Gregory grunted, and Daryna gave a sharp nod.

"And Daryna, even you must see that we must question Gryton. He might be our child just as much as this one." Lillian pointed at her belly, silently reminding Daryna not to start a fight. "And after hearing what you've said about Gryton's upbringing, I do feel some.... responsibility to see if there is something worthy of saving deep in his soul. But that doesn't mean he's innocent or that simply by virtue of his parentage his hands are suddenly washed clean of blood. He's snuffed out a great many innocent lives."

All without a hint of remorse as far as I can see, Lillian thought to herself.

"I still believe he is worthy of being saved and that the Divine Ones have a task for him to perform and ultimately that he was brought about by our creators will. However," Daryna paused to take in the sight of Gregory's lashing tail. "I also understand that you both will need to see what I have seen in him. I am willing to work with you to retrieve our son so that you both may discover what I have already learned."

"And if Lillian and I deem him incurable of the darkness the Battle Goddess has instilled in him?" Gregory's words still managed to have a growling edge to them even though he wasn't actually growling.

"I will not kill our son." The air around Daryna

snapped with rising power. "Nor will I allow either of you to harm our son."

"Easy. If worse comes to worst, I'm still not going to let Gregory kill Gryton," Lillian said.

Gregory huffed in surprise and now watched her with narrowed eyes.

"Think about it, Gregory. The last time Gryton attacked to capture Shadowlight, he didn't kill anyone. I thought it was because he was too weak, but it wasn't that. I think he was trying not to do any lasting harm to his 'victims' this time around."

Daryna nodded as she released the power she'd been gathering back into the surrounding forest where it wouldn't do any harm. "Yes, once I learned a little about Gryton, I came to understand that he finds his actions distasteful but hasn't a choice. Now that I've given him an alternative to the Battle Goddess's harsh rule, he seems willing to embrace it."

"Fine," Gregory said, an actual growl rattling in his tones this time. "I will find Gryton and judge if he's curable. But if darkness runs to his core, I will see him destroyed for the good of all."

Lillian lightly slapped her mate across the muzzle to get his attention. "No. If Gryton can't be saved, then the Divine Ones will get to do the deed. There's no way I'm letting any of us carry that kind of guilt into the next life. Daryna if you have a problem with that, go pick a fight with the Divine Ones."

Daryna looked shocked and appalled. Lillian grinned. She'd had that same effect on Gregory from time to time.

Taking advantage of Daryna's shock, Lillian pressed hard. "Now...start explaining what happened to Shadowlight. You were somehow involved with that. I know you were because Gryton was. Talk. Or else I step back and see what Gregory does."

Daryna's expression underwent a subtle shift, losing much of its earlier confidence.

"I did not intend for Shadowlight to be taken to the Battle Goddess."

"All Gryton's idea?"

"No. I had meant for Shadowlight to go to Lord Death. Once the Lord of the Underworld sees just what his sister is planning, he'll be forced to question the Divine Ones and their choice to allow the Battle Goddess to continue to exist."

"Gregory was concerned what Death would do should he ever get his hands on me. I assume that he would be no more pleased with Shadowlight. So you'd planned to just hand over my little brother...." Lillian fisted her hands and then sought for calm.

Peacekeeper. I'm a peacekeeper.

Marginally calmer, she continued. "Throwing my little brother to the wolves isn't helping your cause."

Daryna turned on her heels and started to pace. It must have been catching.

"It wouldn't have been throwing him to the wolves, as you call it. I've known Lord Death all his existence. He would see past what the Battle Goddess wanted to turn Shadowlight into. He would see Shadowlight's pure soul. He'd never harm the cub."

"That wasn't your choice to make," Gregory growled.

"No. But he needed to be trained. He, too, has a role to play in all this. You know he does."

"He was mine to train."

"No. He was a distraction. Lord Death has thousands of gargoyles. I intended for one of them to train Shadowlight, freeing you for more important things."

"There is nothing more important than a child," Gregory's voice slipped an octave lower.

Lillian squeezed Gregory's arm as she faced Daryna. "What went wrong?"

"I knew Gregory wouldn't part with the cub. Shadowlight means too much to you and Gregory can deny you nothing. Think of me what you will, but Shadowlight needs a mentor who can spend every moment with him. I asked Gryton to take Shadowlight to the edge of Lord Death's domain where the other gargoyles would find him."

"Somehow, that's not what happened," Lillian said with more venom than she'd intended. She couldn't help it. She wasn't a saint, and because of the Mother's Sorceress, Shadowlight was now in enemy hands.

"No. I asked Gryton to call for three of his least liked lieutenants to aid him in capturing Shadowlight. I knew Gregory would make quick work of whoever Gryton summoned. They were to be a distraction only—not a true threat. But many more arrived than we expected and unfortunately that allowed for Shadowlight's capture in truth."

"Your plan sucked." Lillian's talons flexed against her

thigh. "But there's one thing I don't understand. Why did you betray Anna?"

"I did not betray the hybrid. She wished to go. And the cub will need a reason to fight for his freedom. And Anna will be the friend that will get him through a terribly dark time."

"The human will be the mother bear to Shadowlight's cub. But your plan still puts the human at great risk." Some of Gregory's rage diminished as his expression turned thoughtful. "However, I do agree that Anna's arrival in Shadowlight's life is not the result of random chance. I am certain that was Divine will at work. Perhaps this was as well. After all, the Battle Goddess admires two things. Strength and loyalty. Anna possesses them both. She might win the Lady of Battle's admiration and be able to use that against her in some way."

"Oh, lucky Anna," Lillian hissed. "You two are cut from the same cloth."

Gregory looked perplexed, so Lillian explained. "Now the Battle Goddess has them both to torture. She'll use one against the other as leverage. She'll break them both."

"Then she will find she has forged a weapon that will cut the hand that wields it."

"She. Is. Going. To. Torture. Them." Lillian rocked forward onto her talon-tipped toes until she stood muzzle to muzzle with Gregory.

"Yes. The Battle Goddess is not above torture, both physical and spiritual. But as long as there is life, there is hope. The Lady of Battles will not kill them. And I do plan to rescue them. Soon. Just as soon as I get my talons upon

Gryton and we have a 'heart to heart' and I determine if he's as worthy as my other half says he is."

Daryna stepped in closer to Gregory, reaching out to touch the side of his face, but he stepped out of reach.

Allowing her arm to fall back to her side, she tilted her head and her gaze turned vacant for a moment.

"Ah. That might be a bit of a problem as he just resurrected the remains of the spell I created to send Anna to the Magic Realm. He's a quick study."

Gregory snarled something in his native tongue and Lillian didn't blame him.

"Peace. For now, it's better this way. Besides, I still have faith that the human will find a way to free Shadowlight even before Gryton has a chance to aid in their escape. That human is tenacious and lethal. Before I sent her, I made sure she had an honest chance at rescuing the cub."

"What else did you do?" Gregory asked, but sounded tired and like nothing would surprise him anymore.

"I further enhanced her gargoyle bloodline. She won't shift into a full gargoyle for some months yet, but she will be stronger, faster and far more lethal."

"So you gave mamma bear bigger teeth and sharper claws? Are you actually trying to get her killed?" Lillian couldn't help the accusation. Screw being a peacekeeper. She knew Daryna disdained the humans.

Daryna arched an eyebrow. "Do you not know I can read you when we are close and you are angry?"

"Yeah. Well. At least I'm honest."

"You haven't always been honest to Gregory."

Lillian growled and looked at Gregory. "You deal with her. She's your other half."

"It's time we return to Major Resnick and explain to our human allies what you have done. You will no longer have the freedoms you had before. Do you understand what I am saying?" Gregory asked.

Daryna huffed out a sigh. "Yes. And you have my word that as long as you give Gryton a chance, I will not go against your wishes again."

Gregory snorted out a humorless laugh. "Oh, my Sorceress. It's not just me you will have to convince. It is the humans. I have agreed to be their ally and they mine. Thus, I have a few more rules to adhere to than in previous lives. Those humans might see things in a very different light."

"I will tell them the same thing I have told you. If given a choice, Gryton will side with us, and he will be a powerful ally in the fight against the Battle Goddess. And I think the humans will understand the value of having a 'man on the inside' to act as our spy."

"Yeah," Lillian muttered under her breath. "Because double agents are oh so trustworthy."

Daryna glanced in Lillian's direction. "Gryton will side with us. He has no love for the Battle Goddess."

"Maybe," Lillian said grudgingly. "But we're done chatting. It's time to go share this new information with Major Resnick. I'll let him figure out how to word it to his superiors. But after that, we're forming a plan to rescue Shadowlight."

Gregory nodded agreement and then began to summon

spirit magic and directed it into another of those portal spells. She really did need to learn more about magic and see if she could create such a spell. But that was a concern for later. Now, it was time to come clean with the humans.

Daryna stepped up beside Gregory, showing herself to be docile and willing.

Lillian wondered how long that would last if Gregory later met Gryton and didn't agree with Daryna's assessment of their son.

Eyeing the Mother's Sorceress, Lillian couldn't help but think about that clichéd phrase about keeping your friends close and your enemies closer. Somehow, given the situation she found herself in, it seemed like sage advice.

For now, her war with her sorceress self might be over, but the tension was still there, hinting at more war and peril just over the horizon. And come it would. For tomorrow they would begin the hunt for Gryton and find a way to rescue Shadowlight and Anna.

THE END

** Lillian, Gregory, Anna and Shadowlight's story continues in *Sorceress Enraged*. **

** Hey before you go, can I interest you in signing up for my author newsletter? You get my free starter library as a gift for joining. **

http://lisablackwood.com/join-the-newsletter-here/

Did you enjoy Sorceress at War?
If you have a moment and wouldn't mind leaving a review, that would be greatly appreciated. Reviews help other readers to decide if a book is something they would like. It doesn't need to be long. Even a few words is tremendously helpful.

None of this would have been possible without, you, my readers. You're awesome! Thank You!

Bye for now,
Lisa Blackwood

ABOUT THE AUTHOR

Lisa Blackwood is the author of the bestselling Gargoyle and Sorceress urban fantasy series. Her work has also landed on the Wall Street Journal and the USA Today Bestseller lists as part of the Dominion Rising Anthology. When she's not reading and writing, she also enjoys gardening and spending time with her horse and her dogs.

At present, she grudgingly lives in a small town in Southern Ontario, though she would much rather live deep in a dark forest, surrounded by majestic old-growth trees. Since she cannot live her fantasy, she decided to write fantasy instead.

BOOKS BY LISA BLACKWOOD

Gargoyle & Sorceress

Dawn of the Sorceress

Sorceress Awakening

Sorceress Rising

Sorceress Hunting

Sorceress at War

Sorceress Enraged

Legacy of the Sorceress

Sorcery & Firedrakes

Scion of the Sorceress

Sorceress Eternal

In Deception's Shadow Series (Epic Fantasy Romance)

Betrayal's Price

Herd Mistress

Maiden's Wolf

Death's Queen

The Prince's Gryphon (forthcoming)

Ishtar's Legacy Series (Epic Fantasy Romance)

Ishtar's Blade

The Blade's Beginning (short story)

Blade's Honor

Blade's Destiny

The Blade's Shadow

First Queen of the Gryphons

The King of the Anunnaki (forthcoming)

The Anunnaki's Blade (forthcoming)

Huntress vs Huntsman (Fantasy Romance)

Master of the Hunt

Night Huntress

Dragon Archer

Soul Mage (forthcoming)

www.ingramcontent.com/pod-product-compliance
Lightning Source LLC
Chambersburg PA
CBHW030809210726
48290CB00002B/495